# 我的第一本百科

## 親子英語

郭玥慧、邱佳翔
◎合著

親子一起讀最適合「青少年」的英文文章
一起面對各種青春期問題

MP3

### 這本是專為青少年和爸媽設計的英文課外讀物！

- **青少年最關心的主題** 充滿各種問題的青少年生活、最新的自然科學和科技—如何透過Youtube名利雙收、網路銀行、青少年尋找夢想和青少年戀愛。
- **青少年最需要知道的主題** 拓展視野的世界文化和歷史、學校沒教的現代發明—核能發電、谷歌、復活節島和死海。
- **兩大學習架構** 閱讀+選擇題—讀完文章後，馬上練習，選選看「關鍵資訊」！

# Preface
## 作者序

　　對青少年而言，雖然不是人人立志日後成為科學家，但科普與跨領域學習絕對有其必要性。學習此類新知能讓青少年增廣見聞，提升科學涵養。同理，雖然不是人人未來都要擔任英文老師，但英文學習絕對不可輕忽。學習英文能讓青少年接軌國際，以國際語言表達自我。

　　有鑑於上述兩者對於青少年的未來發展極其重要，我負責的 20 個主題，內容涵蓋科技、天文、考古、人文等，讓青少年以閱讀百科全書的方式來提升英文與科學能力。每個單元皆以語意淺顯的短篇文章方式呈現，並附上中文翻譯以供對照，接著列出 10 個詞彙供未來描述相關主題時參考，最後再針對該篇文章列出三題選擇題，讓學習者能檢視自己對文章的理解程度。希望本書能夠讓所有英文學習者以最輕鬆的方式提升自身英文與科普能力。

邱佳翔

　　這本英語百科網羅了各式各樣的主題，盡量貼近青少年的生活與學業，讓年輕讀者可以透過英語得到更多知識或是生活中的幫助，也希望引起青少年的好奇心，有動力去做更多的搜尋與更深入的了解。之後進入高中，將會面對大量不同領域的閱讀測驗，儘早累積各式知識以及閱讀的能力，相信會讓往後的學習更加得心應手。

　　文章的後面還涵蓋了一些閱讀後的問題，讀者可以測試自己閱讀理解與吸收的狀況。我一直希望傳達的是語言是工具，學習英語最重要的還是要拿來使用，在現在這個資訊充斥、訊息取得輕鬆的時代，幾乎所有的知識都可以查得到，所以閱讀只是第一步，更重要的是閱讀之後，是否可以理解，並進一步整理成對自己有意義的資訊，甚至能透過寫作或口述轉達給他人。如果可以透過這本英語百科，多加訓練自己理解、分析、彙整跟轉述的能力，相信會對自己在各方面的表現都非常有幫助。這個世界還有很多知識等著你去開發，希望這本書只是個開始，引導你使用英語去認識這個世界的過去、現在與未來，並練習去彙整這些知識。

郭玥慧

# Editor
## 編者序

「學習英語」讓你得到更多知識,實踐「知識就是力量」。

　　這是一本適合 12-18 歲青少年閱讀的英文生活課本,隨著網路世代的來臨,台灣青少年在英語課上讀到的「英文」,也許早就不能引起他們的興趣了。經歷青春期的孩子們,除了日漸沉重的課業壓力外,生活上也開始面臨不同的壓力—生理和心理的變化。本書特別收錄國中程度的「自然科學」、「科技發展」,貼近「青少年生活」—夢想、戀愛和各種網路議題主題的文章,透過閱讀激發大孩子們的想像力。

　　有別於英文雜誌,本書更深入的探討各個主題的始末,單元「世界文化和歷史」讓孩子們坐在書桌前也能培養國際觀。希望這些精心挑選的文章能夠真正幫助到他們,練習英語閱讀力的同時也得到更多知識,讓他們對事情能有更多的理解和學習,足以面對不管是課業還是生活情緒上的壓力,度過「青春期」這一個充滿酸甜苦辣的人生時期。

# Contents
## 目錄

## Part 2 青少年生活

# Part 3 世界文化和歷史

 **Part 4 現代發明**

# Part 1 自然科學和科技

　　自然科學是研究大自然中有機或是無機的事物和現象的科學。自然科學包括天文學、化學、地球科學和生物學等，藉由兩大重要支柱—對自然的觀察和邏輯推理，歸納出大自然中的規律。科技是人類運用知識、工具和技能來解決存在的問題，也是一種社會變遷的動力。本篇收錄共十四單元—自然科學和科技，自然科學約六篇和科技共八篇，從天文和生物學到最新網路科技應用—Youtube 和網路課程，學英文也拓展孩子課堂外的視野。

# 1-1 Black Hole
## 黑洞

 **Word Bank 天文**

| 字彙 | 音標 | 詞性 | 中譯 |
| --- | --- | --- | --- |
| astronomical | ˌæstrəˋnɑmɪkl | *adj.* | 天文的 |
| enchantment | ɪnˋtʃæntmənt | *n.* | 魅力 |
| gravitational | ˋgrævəˋteʃənl | *adj.* | 重力的 |
| counter | ˋkaʊntɚ | *v.* | 抗衡 |
| essence | ˋɛsns | *n.* | 本質 |
| distort | dɪsˋtɔrt | *v.* | 扭曲 |
| neighborhood | ˋnebɚˌhʊd | *n.* | 鄰近地區 |
| evaporate | ɪˋvæpəˌret | *v.* | 蒸發 |
| verify | ˋvɛrəˌfaɪ | *v.* | 證實 |
| apparent | əˋpærənt | *adj.* | 明顯的 |
| collapse | kəˋlæps | *v.* | 瓦解 |

 **Word Bank**

**Reading—Black Hole**

 MP3 001

### What is a black hole?

What is a black hole? Is it black? Is it a hole? With so much mystery of black holes in our Milky Way Galaxy, such **astronomical** phenomenon (現象) does create mysterious and dangerous images as well as endless **enchantment** and imagination in ordinary people's minds.

### Why is it called the black hole?

The theories of black holes were first proposed by scientists during the mid-eighteenth century. A black hole is a region in space where the **gravitational** (重力的) effects are so strong that nothing, including light, can escape from it. Because light can't be reflected here, this region is like a black body. Therefore, scientists call them "black" holes. A black hole is formed after the death of a star. When dying stars burn up all their energy, they begin to **collapse** under their own weight because there is nothing to **counter** their gravity.

Soon the size of those stars gets extremely small but their density becomes extremely high. Then, they become the black holes. Sincea black hole is still an object, in **essence**, it is not a "hole". Though there is a boundary called the "event

1 自然科學和科技
2 青少年生活
3 世界文化和歷史
4 現代發明

horizon" around, it is not possible to observe a black hole directly. Scientists gain information by observing how a black hole impacts other objects such as its energy emission before entering this region. Then, they can prove black holes do exist and further calculate the mass of them. In accordance with (依據) Einstein's Theory of Relativity, a black hole, due to its massive gravitational influence, **distorts** and the space and time of the **neighborhood**.

**The closer we get to a black hole, the slower time runs.**

For years, scientists try to uncover the mysteries of the black hole. For example, in 1974, Professor Stephen Hawking maintained that black holes would eventually **evaporate** over time. We called his theory "Hawking Radiation." However, it still needs time to **verify** the correctness. Even though some ambiguities remain unsolved, researchers nowadays widely accept that the closer we get to a black hole, the slower time runs. Whatever gets pulled into a black hole can never escape. However, it is only when objects get too close to the black hole that the stronger gravitational force will become **apparent** and pull objects in.

## Multiple Choices 小知識選選看

❶ Which of the following is correct?

(A) Lights can escape from the black holes.

(B) The density of a black hole is high.

(C) Black holes doesn't distort and the space and time of the neighborhood.

❷ The density of a black hole is _____.

(A) high

(B) low

(C) Impossible to measure

❸ When we get closer to the black hole, time goes _____.

(A) faster

(B) slower

(C) as usual

## ▶▶ 文章中譯

### 黑洞是什麼？

什麼是黑洞？黑洞是黑色的嗎？黑洞是一個洞嗎？我們的銀河系中存在著謎團重重的黑洞，這種天文現象在一般人眼中既神秘且危險，但又不免對其充滿無限嚮往與想像。

### 黑洞這個名稱是怎麼來的？

科學家在 18 世紀中期首度提出黑洞理論。黑洞指的是太空中的一個區域，此區域的重力強烈到沒有任何東西，包括光能夠逃離。因為光在此處無法形成反射，這個區域就是像是個黑體。所以科學家將其稱為「黑」洞。恆星死亡後會形成黑洞，當垂死的恆星將其能量燃燒殆盡時，由於沒有任何東西能與其重力抗衡，它們便會開始因著自己的重量而瓦解。

很快地，恆星的體積變得非常小，但密度變得非常大，接著就成為了黑洞。由於在本質上還是物體，所以黑洞其實不是一個「洞」。雖然在黑洞周圍有「事件視界」這樣的邊界，直接觀測黑洞仍然是不可能的任務。科學家透過觀察黑洞如何影響其他物體，例如進入黑洞前的能量釋放來獲得相關資訊；接著他們就能證實黑洞確實存在，並計算其質量。根據愛因斯坦的相對論，由於黑洞本身具有強大的重力，它會扭曲附近的時間與空間。

### 當我們越接近黑洞，時間就流逝的越緩慢。

許多年以來，科學家嘗試解開黑洞的謎團。舉例來說，史蒂芬霍金教授在 1974 年提出黑洞終將隨時間蒸發的說法，這個理論被稱為

「霍金輻射」，然而此理論正確與否仍有待時間來驗證。儘管目前仍有些矛盾之處尚未找到解答，一般說來，今日學者普遍接受一個觀點：當我們越接近黑洞，時間就流逝的越緩慢。任何被拉進黑洞中的物體永遠無法逃脫；但是唯有當物體太靠近黑洞時，強烈的重力才會顯露出它的力量並把物體拉進去。

## ▶▶ 選擇題中譯

❶ 以下何者正確？

(A) 光線可以逃離黑洞

(B) 黑洞的密度很高

(C) 黑洞不會扭曲鄰近的空間與時間

❷ 黑洞的密度是？

(A) 高

(B) 低

(C) 無法測量

❸ 當我們越靠近黑洞，時間會變得_____。

(A) 更快

(B) 更慢

(C) 一如往常

選擇題答案：1.B　2.A　3.B

1 自然科學和科技

2 青少年生活

3 世界文化和歷史

4 現代發明

# 1-2 Halley's Comet
## 哈雷彗星

 **Word Bank 哈雷彗星**

| 字彙 | 音標 | 詞性 | 中譯 |
|---|---|---|---|
| heavenly | ˋhɛvənlɪ | adj. | 天空的 |
| period | ˋpɪrɪəd | n. | 時期 |
| track | træk | n. | 軌跡 |
| commend | kəˋmɛnd | v. | 表揚 |
| visible | ˋvɪzəb! | adj. | 可看見的 |
| probe | prob | n. | 探測器 |
| nucleus | ˋnjuklɪəs | n. | 核心 |
| coma | ˋkomə | n. | 彗髮 |
| omen | ˋomən | n. | 預兆 |
| awe | ɔ | v. | 敬畏 |

**Word Bank**

# Reading–Halley 's Comet

MP3 002

Though comets are rarely seen in the sky, they are important **heavenly** bodies of the solar system. Among them, Halley's Comet is probably the most famous one. It is the only known short-**period** comet that is **visible** with the naked eye from Earth. It returns every 75 to 76 years. If you are lucky enough, you might see it twice in your lifetime.

## The Earliest Track of Halley's Comet

The earliest **track** of Halley's Comet can be dated back as far as 240 BC. The Clear records of the comet's appearances were made by the astronomers in Chinese, Babylonian, and medieval European. However, none of them regarded it as the reappearance of the same comet at that time. In 1705, an English astronomer, Edmund Halley, first recognized the comet's regular and periodic appearances. Therefore, the comet is named after Halley to **commend** his contribution.

## It is like a "dirty snowball".

In 1986, the year of Halley's Comet's previous perihelion (近日點) passage, scientists observed this comet in detail for the first time. Using space **probes** of several different countries, the structure of its **nucleus**, the mechanism of **coma** and tail formation were further observed and confirmed. According to

自然科學和科技

青少年生活

世界文化和歷史

現代發明

astronomers, Halley's Comet is probably composed of water, carbon dioxide (二氧化碳), ammonia(氨), dust, etc. and it is icy in a portion like a "dirty snowball".

Halley's Comet has long been thought to be a bad **omen** by some scientist and has been **awed** by the general public who believes such saying for great disasters and unfavorable changes might take place after its appearances; most of us still look forward to the coming of 2061 when Halley's Comet is predicted to reappear.

## Multiple Choices 小知識選選看

❶ For people nowadays, how many times the most can they see the Halley's Comet?
(A) one time
(B) two times
(C) three times

❷ When do scientists have the opportunity to observe Halley's Comet in detail?
(A) 240 BC
(B) 1705
(C) 1986

❸ Why did scientists call Halley's Comet "a dirty snowball"?
(A) it is made of water, carbon dioxide, ammonia, dust, etc
(B) a small portion of it is icy
(C) all of above

1　自然科學和科技

2　青少年生活

3　世界文化和歷史

4　現代發明

## ▶▶ 文章中譯

　　雖然彗星在天空中很罕見，但它們卻是太陽系中很重要的天體。在眾多彗星中，尤以哈雷彗星最為知名。哈雷彗星是目前唯一可從地球以肉眼觀察到的短週期彗星，其週期為 75 至 76 年。如果你夠幸運的話，一生之中可以看到哈雷彗星兩次。

### 哈雷彗星最早的軌跡

　　天文學家對哈雷彗星的軌跡追蹤最早可追溯至西元前 240 年。舉凡中國、巴比倫與中世紀的歐洲，都對此彗星留下清楚的紀錄，但當時並不認為這是同一顆彗星再次出現。時至 1705 年，英國天文學家艾德蒙•哈雷首次推斷該彗星會規律且定期地出現。為了表揚哈雷的貢獻，該彗星就以他的名字命名。

### 它就像一個「骯髒的雪球」

　　在 1986 年，也就是上一次哈雷彗星最靠近太陽的那年，科學家們首次仔細觀察這顆彗星。透過不同國家的太空探測器，舉凡哈雷彗星彗核的結構、彗髮的構成，以及彗尾的組成，皆得以進一步地觀察並確認。根據天文學家的說法，哈雷彗星很可能是由水、二氧化碳、氨、塵埃等成分所組成，且有一小部分是結凍的，就像是一顆「骯髒雪球」。

　　儘管哈雷彗星長久以來被部分科學家視為一種惡兆，且被相信此說法的社會大眾所敬畏著，認為哈雷彗星的出現會招來大災難或是不良的改變，但多數人仍舊期待 2061 年的到來，也就是哈雷彗星被預期再次出現的那年。

## ▶▶ 選擇題中譯

❶ 對今日的人們來說，一生中最多可以看到幾次哈雷彗星？

(A) 一次

(B) 兩次

(C) 三次

❷ 何時科學家才有機會仔細觀察哈雷彗星？

(A) 西元前 240 年

(B) 西元 1705 年

(C) 西元 1986 年

❸ 為何科學家稱哈雷彗星為「骯髒雪球」？

(A) 它是由水、二氧化碳、氨、塵埃等所組成

(B) 它有一小部分是結凍的

(C) 以上皆是

選擇題答案：1.B　2.C　3.C

# 1-3 Pluto
## 冥王星

 **Word Bank** 冥王星

| 字彙 | 音標 | 詞性 | 中譯 |
|------|------|------|------|
| deem | dim | v. | 認為 |
| underworld | ˋʌndɚˏwɝld | n. | 地獄 |
| rotate | ˋrotet | v. | 旋轉 |
| atmosphere | ˋætməsˏfɪr | n. | 大氣層 |
| satellite | ˋsæt!ˏaɪt | n. | 衛星 |
| revolution | ˏrɛvəˋluʃən | n. | 公轉 |
| dwarf | dwɔrf | n. | 侏儒 |
| orbit | ˋɔrbɪt | n. | 運行軌道 |
| vacancy | ˋvekənsɪ | n. | 空缺 |

**Word Bank**

**Reading–Pluto**

 MP3 003

Though Pluto is the planet which is furthest from the sun in the solar system, it hasn't always remained remain mysterious. It is common sense that Pluto was the last to be found among the nine planets for the most general public nowadays. Surprisingly, such a saying has been overturned by new scientific evidence. Pluto is no longer **deemed** an official planet.

The name of this planet perfectly matches its appearance. Pluto was found by a 24-year-old American research assistant, Clyde Tombaugh in 1930. Meanwhile, an eleven-year-old girl Venetia Burney named it Pluto, the Roman god of the **Underworld** because of its similar images of the Underworld and the planet. The previous one is far away from the Earth; the latter **rotates** at the furthest reaches of the sun. Pluto is believed to have a thick methane (沼氣) **atmosphere** about a few kilometers deep and is covered with frost and ice. During the 1970s, astronomers discovered that both Pluto and its **satellite**, Charon completed a **revolution** about six to seven days by themselves and the two are almost the same size. As a result, sometimes astronomers refer to them as double planets.

**It is not an official planet anymore.**

Though regarded as an "official" planet for 76 years, Pluto was renamed a "**Dwarf** Planet" in 2006, due to the new discovery that it is merely the brightest member of the Kuiper Belt, a mass of objects that **orbit** the sun beyond Neptune (海王星). Therefore, we can only say that there are eight planets in the solar system unless scientists find a new planet to make up the **vacancy** left by Pluto.

**Molecule**

## Multiple Choices 小知識選選看

❶ Which of the following is correct?
(A) Pluto is found in the 1970s
(B) The name of Pluto comes from Roman Underground God
(C) The atmosphere of Pluto is thin

❷ Why Pluto doesn't be regarded as an official planet now?
(A) it is merely the brightest member of the Kuiper Belt
(B) it is not inside solar system
(C) it is too small

❸ How long does Pluto need to finish one revolution?
(A) 2-3 days
(B) 4-5 days
(C) 6-7 days

雖然冥王星是太陽系中離太陽最遠的行星，但我們對它並非總是一無所知。今日多數人都知道它是九大行星中最後一個被發現的。但令人驚訝的是，此說法已被新的科學證據所推翻，冥王星不再被視為九大行星的一員。

冥王星可謂名實相符。在 1930 年，一名 24 歲的美國研究助理，克萊德‧湯博發現了冥王星；與此同時，一名 11 歲大的女孩，薇妮第‧伯納以羅馬冥界之神為其命名為冥王星，因為這顆星球上的景像酷似冥界的場景。後者離人世間相當遙遠，前者則於離太陽最遙遠的地方旋轉著。冥王星據悉擁有約幾公里厚，由濃密甲烷組成的大氣層，且表面被霜和冰覆蓋著。在 1970 年代，天文學家發現冥王星和它的衛星查倫，完成一次公轉需要 6~7 天左右，而且這兩顆行星幾乎大小相同，所以有時候天文學家稱呼它們為雙行星。

**它不再是九大行星的一員了**

冥王星雖然被視為九大行星的一員長達 76 年，但是在 2006 年它被重新命名為「矮行星」，因為最新發現顯示它只是古柏帶，也就是在海王星外環繞太陽軌道運轉的一群行星體中最亮的一顆星球。因此，除非科學家發現新的行星來補足冥王星所留下的空缺，否則我們現在只能說太陽系有八大行星。

▶▶ **選擇題中譯**

❶ 以下何者正確？

(A) 冥王星於 1970 年代時被發現

(B) 冥王星之名源於羅馬冥界之神

(C) 冥王星的大氣層很薄

❷ 為何冥王星現在不再被視為九大行星的一員？

(A) 它僅是古柏帶內最亮的星體

(B) 它不在太陽系內

(C) 它的體積太小了

❸ 冥王星自轉一周要多久？

(A) 2 至 3 天

(B) 4 至 5 天

(C) 6 至 7 天

選擇題答案：1.B　2.A　3.C

# 1-4 Newton's Three Laws of Motion
## 牛頓三大運動定律

 **Word Bank 牛頓三大運動定律**

| 字彙 | 音標 | 詞性 | 中譯 |
| --- | --- | --- | --- |
| brilliant | `brɪljənt | adj. | 才華洋溢的 |
| depreciate | dɪ`priʃɪˌet | v. | 看輕 |
| motion | `moʃən | n. | 運動 |
| recognition | ˌrɛkəg`nɪʃən | n. | 認知 |
| friction | `frɪkʃən | n. | 摩擦 |
| acceleration | ækˌsɛlə`reʃən | n. | 加速度 |
| proportional | prə`porʃən! | adj. | 成比例的 |
| mass | mæs | n. | 質量 |
| mechanism | `mɛkəˌnɪzəm | n. | 機制 |

**Word Bank**

##  **Reading—The Three Laws of Motions**

🔊 MP3 004

Isaac Newton is one of the most outstanding scientists in history. Though he was **brilliant**; he was a humble person who always tried to **depreciate** his contributions to science. He once remarked, "If I have seen further than others, it is by standing upon the shoulders of Giants. However, the three laws of **motion** he formulated in the 17th century did greatly affect scientific development in the following centuries.

The first law of motion refers to any change in the motion of an object from the result of a force. In the 17th century, people believed that it was natural for moving objects to slow down and eventually stop moving. As a result, the concept Newton proposed greatly challenged the mainstream **recognition** of motion at that time. Today, we know that an object slows down and stops because of the force of **friction**. According to this logic, unless an object is put into space without the force of friction, Newton's first law always proves to be right.

The second law of motion describes changes in speed. Acceleration is directly **proportional** to the amount of force applied and inversely proportional to **mass**. Simply speaking, the more force you apply to an object, the higher the value of

自然科學和科技　1

青少年生活　2

世界文化和歷史　3

現代發明　4

**acceleration**. On the contrary, the heavier an object is, the lower the value of acceleration when a force is applied.

The third law of motion states that there is always an equal and opposite reaction to every action you take. In other words, there is a **mechanism** to maintain the balance between an object and the force applied to it in nature. You can imagine you are stepping off a boat that is not securely moored (固定). As you try to move forward, the boat moves backward. That is how the third law of motion works.

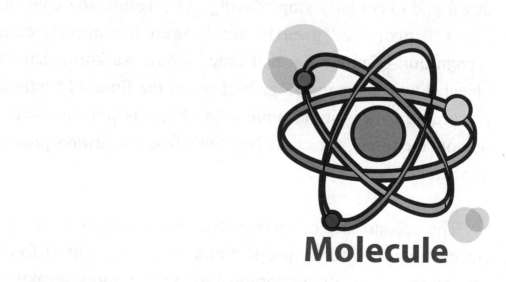

**Molecule**

## Multiple Choices 小知識選選看

❶ A moving object will slow down and stop because of the force of _____.
(A) friction
(B) acceleration
(C) gravity

❷ Acceleration is proportional to _____.
(A) the amount of the force
(B) mass
(C) nothing

❸ When a force is applied to an object, the will be a(n) _____ and _____ reaction to the force.
(A) bigger; opposite
(B) smaller; opposite
(C) equal; opposite

## ▶▶ 文章中譯

　　以撒•牛頓是史上最傑出的科學家之一。他雖然很聰明，但為人十分謙虛。牛頓總是輕看自己在科學上的貢獻，他曾說過「如果說我看得比別人遠，是因為我站在巨人的肩膀上。」但他 17 世紀所提出的三大運動定律大大影響接下來幾世紀的科學發展。

　　第一運動定律談到物體有任何運動改變皆是因外力使然。17 世紀時，人們普遍相信移動的物體終將速度變慢，最後自然停止；因此牛頓提出的概念徹底挑戰了當時對物體運動的主流認知。今日我們都知道運動中的物體會因摩擦力而減速及停止。依照此邏輯，除非將物體放到沒有摩擦力的空間，否則牛頓第一運動定律永遠都是正確的。

　　牛頓第二運動定律談到速度的改變。加速度與施力成正比，與質量成反比。簡單來說，施加在物體上的力越大，加速度值就越高。相反地，當物體質量越大，物體受力時加速度值就越低。

　　牛頓第三運動定律談到每個動作都會產生一個大小相等且方向相反的反作用力。換言之，自然界中存在一種機制，得以維持物體與施加於其上力量的平衡。試想如果你現在想從一艘沒有栓好的船下船，你越是想往前走，船就越往後退，這就是因為牛頓第三運動定律的原理。

## ▶▶ 選擇題中譯

❶ 移動中的物體速度會漸慢，最後靜止是因為_____的作用。

(A) 摩擦力

(B) 加速度

(C) 重力

❷ 加速度與_____成正比。

(A) 力的大小

(B) 物體質量

(C) 不與任何物體

❸ 當在物體上施力，必會產生一個_____且_____的力。

(A) 更大；方向相反

(B) 更小；方向相反

(C) 相等；方向相反

選擇題答案：1.A　2.A　3.C

# 1-5 DNA
## 基因密碼—脫氧核糖核酸

 **Word Bank DNA**

| 字彙 | 音標 | 詞性 | 中譯 |
|---|---|---|---|
| spiral | `spaɪrəl | *adj.* | 螺旋的 |
| blueprint | `blu`prɪnt | *n.* | 藍圖 |
| cell | sɛl | *n.* | 細胞 |
| trait | tret | *n.* | 特徵 |
| experiment | ɪk`spɛrəmənt | *n.* | 實驗 |
| factor | `fæktɚ | *n.* | 因素 |
| identify | aɪ`dɛntə‚faɪ | *v.* | 識別 |
| research | rɪ`sɝtʃ | *n.* | 研究 |
| protein | `protin | *n.* | 蛋白質 |
| discovery | dɪs`kʌvərɪ | *n.* | 發現 |

**Word Bank**

## Reading-DNA

 MP3 005

So, have you ever wondered what decides whether you have dark or light skin, or what kinds of diseases one might get? The answers all lie in the DNA or Deoxyribonucleic acid. DNA is a long **spiral** molecule (分子) that contains our genetic code, which can be seen as the **blueprint** of all living things. It lies in the center of **cell**s that tells the chemicals in our bodies when and how to build cells.

**Gregor Mendel – the father of genetics.**

People had long noticed that certain **trait**s of animals or plants, such as height or color, would be passed to the next generation. However, for a while, people were not sure how. Gregor Mendel, who lived in what is now the Czech Republic, did **experiment**s using peas that helped him find out the answer. After nine years of crossbreeding (雜交育種) pea plants and recording his observations, he concluded that there are **factor**s that controlled what traits the offspring would get and some factors are dominant while some are recessive(隱性). The factors are what we now know as "genes." Gregor Mendel is now known as the father of genetics.

**The finding history of "Nuclein"**

In 1869, a Swiss physician and biologist named Friedrich Miescher discovered a new molecule (分子) from blood cells and thus became the first person to isolate and **identify** DNA.

He called what he found at the time "nuclein." (核素) He knew his finding was important and continued to **research** nuclein until he passed away. Unfortunately, no one realized the importance of nuclein then and all the scientists at the time, thought that **protein**s were the carriers of genetic information.

It was not until 1944 that Oswald Avery and his colleagues discovered that DNA carried genes, not protein. In 1953, James Watson and Francis Crick together discovered the double-helix structure (雙股螺旋結構) of DNA and answered the question of how genetic information could be passed on. They received a Nobel Prize for their contribution to the field of DNA.

**We aren't so different from vegetables and animals.**

Watson and Crick's **discovery** has led to a great number of medical and biological advancements. Understanding DNA helps us in many ways, such as solving crimes, predicting diseases, or curing diseases. In 2003, all 3 billion units of human DNA were finally decoded (解碼). This was done relatively quickly because people have very similar genes with animals and all human beings share around 99.9% of the same genes. Interestingly, human beings share around 50% or more of the same genes with cabbages or bananas. It seems like people are not so different from other vegetables or animals.

# Multiple Choices 小知識選選看

_____ ❶ What does the article say about DNA?

(A) DNA decides how and when chemicals form cells.

(B) Miescher discovered that DNA carried genetic information.

(C) People and animals have very different genes.

_____ ❷ How many years did it take for people to identify all human genes after DNA was first isolated and identified?

(A) 134

(B) 59

(C) 9

_____ ❸ Which of the following ways of using DNA is NOT mentioned in this article?

(A) Testing the DNA samples of a man and see if he is involve in a crime.

(B) Changing the DNA of vegetables so they can grow more quickly.

(C) Running a genetic test on a baby to see what kind of diseases the baby may have in the future.

## ▶▶ 文章中譯

你是否曾想過到底是什麼在決定你的膚色是深或淺，或是一個人可能會得到哪些疾病？答案就在也稱作「去氧核糖核酸」的 DNA 裡面。DNA 是一種包含基因密碼的長螺旋分子，而這個密碼也可以看作是所有生物的設計藍圖，DNA 位於細胞核內告訴身體裡的化學物質要在什麼時間還有如何製造細胞。

### 格雷戈爾・孟德爾－遺傳學之父

人們長久以來都有注意到動物或植物的某些特徵，像是高度或顏色等會傳給下一代，然而有很長的一段時間，人們不確定遺傳是如何發生的。住在現在捷克共和國的格雷戈爾・孟德爾使用碗豆做了能幫助他找出答案的實驗。經過九年將碗豆進行雜交育種並記錄觀察結果之後，他的結論是：有些因素會控制後代得到的特徵，而這些特徵有些是顯性，有些則是隱性的。這些因素就是我們現在所知道的「基因」，格雷戈爾・孟德爾現在被稱為「遺傳學之父」。

### 「核素」的發現

在 1869 年，一位名叫弗雷德里希•米歇爾的瑞士醫生兼生物學家在血球裡面發現了新的分子，成為第一位分離並辨識出 DNA 的人，當時他將自己發現的分子稱為「核素」，他知道自己有了重大的發現，因此直到過世前都持續研究著核素。可惜的是，當時沒人看出米歇爾發現的重要性，而且當時所有的科學家，包括米歇爾都認為攜帶基因資訊的應該是蛋白質。

一直到 1944 年奧斯華・艾弗里和他的同事才發現攜帶遺傳因子的是 DNA，不是蛋白質。在 1953 年，詹姆斯・華生與法蘭西斯・克里克為 DNA 研究開啟了十分重要的歷史新頁，他們發現 DNA 的雙股螺旋結構，並找到基因資訊如何遺傳的解答；兩人因為在 DNA 領域的貢獻得到了諾貝爾獎。

**我們和蔬菜還有動物之間並沒有那麼不同**

　　華生與克里克的發現造就了許多醫學和生物學上的進展，了解 DNA 在各方面對我們都很有助益，這可以幫助我們破案、預期疾病或醫治疾病。在 2003 年，人類的三十億組 DNA 終於全數解碼成功，這項工作能快速地完成，是因為人類和動物的基因非常相近，而所有人類的基因有百分之 99.9 是相同的，有趣的是人類和高麗菜以及香蕉的基因有百分之 50 以上相同，看起來人類和其他蔬菜或動物並沒有那麼不同。

## ▶ 選擇題中譯

❶ 文章如何述說 DNA?

　(A) DNA 決定化學物質在何時以及如何形成細胞？

　(B) 米歇發現 DNA 攜帶基因訊息。

　(C) 人類和動物的基因非常不同。

- - - - - - - - - - - - - - - - - - - - - - - - - - - - - - - - - -

❷ 從人們第一次分離並辨識出 DNA 到辨別出所有人類基因為止，共花了多少時間？

　(A) 134 年

　(B) 59 年

　(C) 9 年

- - - - - - - - - - - - - - - - - - - - - - - - - - - - - - - - - -

❸ 文章沒有提及以下哪個使用 DNA 的方法？

　(A) 鑑定一個男人的 DNA 樣本，來看他有沒有犯案。

　(B) 改變植物的 DNA，讓它們長得更快。

　(C) 檢驗一個嬰兒的 DNA，判斷嬰兒未來可能會得到哪些疾病。

- - - - - - - - - - - - - - - - - - - - - - - - - - - - - - - - - -

選擇題答案：1.A　2.A　3.B

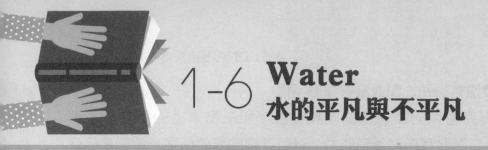

# 1-6 **Water**
## 水的平凡與不平凡

## Word Bank 水

| 字彙 | 音標 | 詞性 | 中譯 |
|---|---|---|---|
| oxygen | `ɑksədʒən | n. | 氧氣 |
| gravity | `grævətɪ | n. | 重力 |
| transport | `træns‚pɔrt | v. | 運輸 |
| attract | ə`trækt | v. | 吸引 |
| pull | pʊl | v. | 拉 |
| stick | stɪk | v. | 黏住 |
| insect | `ɪnsɛkt | n. | 偏見 |
| surface | 'sɜː.fɪs | n. | 表面 |
| float | flot | v. | 漂浮 |
| detergent | dɪ`tɜ-dʒənt | n. | 洗潔劑 |

Word Bank

# Reading–Water

 MP3 006

Over 70 percent of the world is covered by water and the adult human body is about 60 percent water. Water is essential to the human body's survival. Knowing the importance of water, most of early civilization settled near water sources. Water is a small yet amazing thing. Through experiments, British scientist Henry Cavendish was the first person to recognize hydrogen gas as a discrete substance. He also established that water is made of two parts of hydrogen and one part of **oxygen**. That is why water is known as H2O. Each water molecule has a V shape and the oxygen (氧) atom is slightly negative and the hydrogen (氫) atoms are slightly positive. This gives water many interesting characteristics.

**Water can move upward against gravity.**

One of the characteristics of water is that it can move upward against **gravity**. We have all learned that plants **transport** water from their roots to their leaves. Have you ever wondered how? Plants have small vessels in their stems. Since water molecules (分子) are **attract**ed to other molecules, water molecules will be **pull**ed toward vessel walls. In addition, water molecules like to **stick** to each other because of the negative oxygen and positive hydrogen. The positive hydrogens atoms in one water molecule will pull the negative

自然科學和科技　**1**

青少年生活　**2**

世界文化和歷史　**3**

現代發明　**4**

oxygen atoms in the next water molecule (positive and negative attract).

## An Example of Water Moving Upward

Water can move upwards. Similar things happen in our blood vessels. Water's property of that water molecules like to stick together also makes it possible for some **insect**s and even bigger animals to walk on water. Water molecules that bond together contribute to **surface** tension (表面張力). The water molecules on the surface cling (依附) tightly to each other something like a stretched sheet, supporting the insects or animals. This is also why one tends to get really hurt when falls into water from a very high place. Although surface tension is a property common to all liquids, water has a higher surface tension than any other liquid. Try to gently place a needle on the surface of the water to feel the surface tension.

While surface tension serves insects well, it may pose a problem for you when you try to do your laundry. First of all, surface tension prevents your clothes from becoming completely wet. Secondly, things like oil do not like water because they are rather "neutral," (中性) meaning they are not positive or negative. This is why when we try to add oil into water, oil will **float** on the top. Using water will not wash these things away. You need help from the **detergent**.

A substance (物質) added in the detergent we use has two

ends. One end is attracted to water while the other is attracted to oil and it is hydrophobic (疏水的), water fearing. Therefore, the oil can be washed away with water. The hydrophobic end also helps break the surface tension of water. Back to your needle on the water. If you add in enough detergent, the needle will suddenly sink to the bottom of the water. Try it out!

## Multiple Choices 小知識選選看

_____ ❶ Which of the following does not seem to help water move from roots to leaves?

(A) Water molecules like to bond together.

(B) Water molecules are often pulled by other substances.

(C) Water molecules form high surface tension.

_____ ❷ Which of the fact about water molecules is correct?

(A) Water molecules are composed of the attraction between positive hydrogens and negative oxygens.

(B) Water molecules do not bond together as tightly as the molecules in other liquid.

(C) Water molecules are attracted to each other as well as other substances that are not "neutral".

## ▶▶ 文章中譯

　　地球表面超過百分之 70 被水覆蓋，而成人身體裡有百分之 60 是水份，人體要存活的話，水絕對是必要的。就是因為知道水的重要，大部分的早期文化都建立在水源附近。水是個很小，但卻十分神奇的東西。透過實驗，英國科學家亨利・卡文迪成為第一個辨識出氫氣是單一個別元素的人，他也發現水是由兩個氫原子和一個氧原子所構成，所以我們也稱水為 $H_2O$。每個水分子都形成一個 V 的形狀，而它的氧原子偏負極，氫原子則偏正極，這讓水擁有很多有趣的特性。

**水能向上移動，抵抗重力。**

　　水的其中一個特質，就是它能抵抗重力，向上移動。我們都有學過，植物會將水從根部運送到葉子，但你有想過這是怎麼辦到的嗎？植物的莖部有細小的導管，因為水分子會被其他分子吸引，所以水分子會被拉往導管壁，再加上負極氧原子與正極氫原子會讓水分子互相吸引，一個水分子裡的正極氫原子會拉近另一個水分子裡的負極氧原子（正負相吸）。

**水向上移動的例子**

　　因此水可以向上移動，在我們的血管裡，情況也十分類似。同時，也因為水分子互相吸引的特質，昆蟲或甚至稍大一點的動物才有可能在水面上行走。結合在一起的水分子會形成表面張力，在表面的水分子會緊密吸附彼此，就好像一張被拉緊的床單一樣，可以支撐在上面行走的昆蟲或動物。這也是為什麼當人從很高的地方掉到水裡，總是會傷得非常嚴重。雖然表面張力是所有液體共同的特徵，但是水的表面張力可是全部液體裡面最高的。下次試試看輕輕的把針放在水面上，感受一下水的表面張力吧！雖然表面張力讓昆蟲可以輕鬆在水上走，但是你想洗衣服的時候可就麻煩了。首先，表面張力讓衣服沒辦法完全浸濕。其次，像油之類的東西不喜歡水，因為它們是「非極性」的，也就是說既不屬於正極也不屬於負極，所以當我們把油加進水裡的時候，油會浮在表面。所以用水是沒辦法把油汙洗掉的，你需要清潔劑的幫忙。

　　在我們使用的清潔劑裡，有加一種物質，這種物質有兩端，一端親水，另一端則親油且疏水，也就是怕水，油才能因此被水沖掉。疏水的那端也會幫助破壞水的表面張力。回到你剛剛放在水面的針，如果你加入足夠的清潔劑，那根針會突然沉到水底，快去試試看吧！

### ▶▶ 選擇題中譯

❶ 以下哪個選項的描述不能幫助水從根部移動到葉子？

(A) 水分子喜歡連結在一起。

(B) 水分子經常被其他物質吸引。

(C) 水分子能形成強大的表面張力。

❷ 以下哪個關於水分子的描述是正確的？

(A) 水是由氫原子和氧原子正負相吸所組成的。

(B) 水分子不像其他液體中的分子那樣緊密地彼此連結。

(C) 水分子互相吸引，也吸引其他「非極性」的物質。

選擇題答案：1.C　2.A

# 1-7 Online Banking
## 網路銀行

 **Word Bank 網路銀行**

| 字彙 | 音標 | 詞性 | 中譯 |
| --- | --- | --- | --- |
| brick-and-mortar | brɪk—ænd—`mɔrtə | adj. | 實體的 |
| remittance | rɪ`mɪtns | n. | 匯款 |
| clicks | klɪk | n. | 點擊 |
| innovative | `ɪno͵vetɪv | adj. | 創新的 |
| hesitant | `hɛzətənt | adj. | 遲疑的 |
| scale | skel | n. | 規模 |
| transactions | træn`zækʃən | n. | 交易 |
| mainstream | `men͵strim | n. | 主流 |
| widespread | `waɪd͵sprɛd | adj. | 廣泛的 |
| competitive | kəm`pɛtətɪv | adj. | 有競爭力的 |

**Word Bank**

## Reading–Online Banking

 MP3 007

Thanks to the development of the World Wide Web, the definition of banks is no longer limited to a **brick-and-mortar** financial institution. It also means an online commercial service provider in today's high tech world. From **remittance** to investment, people nowadays can finish all these works within a few **clicks** on the Internet instead of actually going to bank to wait in line.

### The online banking problem - the security feature

The concept of online banking became actually accessible (可以使用的) in the 1980s. In 1981, the four biggest banks in New York City Citi Bank, Chase Manhattan, Chemical, and Manufactures Hanover provided home banking service to their customers. However, this **innovative** service didn't strike a chord (引起共鳴) with most at first. Most customers were **hesitant** to use online banking because they didn't trust its security features.

In term of the business **scale** of credit unions, it was relatively small compared to that of big commercial banks. But they are famous for their advanced services in the history of the development of online banking. For example, in the early 1980s, Stanford Federal Credit Union introduced ATMs and banking by phone to their customers.

自然科學和科技　1

青少年生活　2

世界文化和歷史　3

現代發明　4

The real success of online banking began in the mid-1990s. In 1993, Stanford Federal Credit Union conducted its first four internet **transactions**. It became the first financial institution to offer online banking to all of its customers in 1994. One year later, President Bank followed. Soon, e-commerce became the **mainstream**. Therefore, many banks caught on. By the year 2000, 80 percent of banks in the US offered online banking services. Take Bank of America for example, It gained more than 3 million online banking customers in 2001. This figure accounts for 20 percent of its total customer base.

Now online banking service have become even more **widespread** all over the world. For investors, this service allows them to operate their assets (財產) around the world with no time difference issues. For bank owners, online banking effectively decreases the overhead costs to offer more **competitive** rates and enjoy high-profit margins.

## 👓 Multiple Choices 小知識選選看

❶ Online banking becomes widespread because of the development of ＿＿＿＿.
(A) World Wide Web
(B) Telephones
(C) ATMs

❷ Most customers were hesitant to use online banking service in the early 1980s because ＿＿＿＿.
(A) The procedure is too complicated.
(B) They didn't trust its safety feature.
(C) They like to wait in line.

❸ What is the benefit of online banking?
(A) To save investors time
(B) To decrease banks owners overhead cost
(C) All of above

## ▶▶ 文章中譯

隨著網際網路的發展，銀行的定義不再僅侷限於實體金融機構。在當今高科技的世界裡，銀行也可以指線上金融服務的提供者。從匯款到投資，現在人們不必實際去銀行排隊，只要輕鬆地在網路上點擊幾下，就可以完成所有操作。

**因著對網路銀行的服務安全存有疑慮，客戶持觀望態度**

網路銀行的概念始於 1980 年代。在 1981 年，紐約的四大銀行：花旗銀行、大通銀行、美華銀行與漢華實業銀行都提供家庭銀行服務給其客戶。但這項創新的服務一開始並未獲得共鳴，客戶們對於使用網路銀行保持觀望，因為它們對此服務安全性有所疑慮。

就企業規模而言，信用合作社遠不如大型商業銀行。但在線上銀行的發展史中，信用合社可是以提供先進服務聞名。舉例來說，史丹佛聯邦信用合作社在 1980 年代早期就推出自動提款機與電話銀行。

網路銀行至 1990 年代中期才真正普及。在 1993 年，史丹佛聯邦信用合作社進行了該公司的前四筆網路交易，並於 1994 年成為第一個提供網路銀行服務的金融機構。一年後，總統銀行選擇跟進。很快地，電子商務成為主流，許多銀行紛紛迎頭趕上。時至 2000 年，全美有超過百分之八十的銀行提供線上銀行服務。以美國銀行為例，2001 年時該銀行有超過 300 萬的網路銀行客戶，這個數字佔了其總客戶數的百分之二十。

今日網路銀行服務已遍佈全球。對投資者來說，此服務讓他們能夠隨時在世界各地營運資產而無需考慮時差。對銀行經營者來說，此服務能讓他們有效降低營運成本，提供更具競爭力的價格，同時享有更高的利潤。

今日線上銀行服務已遍佈全球。對投資者來說，此服務讓他們能夠隨時在世界各地營運資產，無需考慮時差。對銀行經營者來說，此服務能讓有效降低營運成本，提供更具競爭力的價格，同時享有更高的利潤。

## ▶▶ 選擇題中譯

❶ 網路銀行變得很普遍是因為＿＿＿＿的發展。

(A) 網路

(B) 電話

(C) ATM

❷ 在 1980 年代，大部分的客戶對網路銀行的使用保持觀望，因為＿＿＿＿＿。

(A) 使用程序太複雜。

(B) 人們不相信它的安全性。

(C) 人們喜歡去排隊。

❸ 以下哪一個是網路銀行的優點？

(A) 節省投資人的時間。

(B) 減少銀行營運者的營運成本。

(C) 以上皆是。

選擇題答案：1.A　2.B　3.C

1 自然科學和科技

2 青少年生活

3 世界文化和歷史

4 現代發明

# 1-8 Google 谷歌

## Word Bank 谷歌

| 字彙 | 音標 | 詞性 | 中譯 |
| --- | --- | --- | --- |
| influence | ˋɪnflʊəns | n. | 影響力 |
| accessible | ækˋsɛsəb! | adj. | 可取得的 |
| browser | ˋbraʊzɚ | n. | 瀏覽器 |
| comprehensive | ͵kamprɪˋhɛnsɪv | adj. | 全面性的 |
| orientation | ͵orɪɛnˋteʃən | n. | 新生訓練 |
| disagreement | ͵dɪsəˋgrimənt | n. | 意見不合 |
| suspend | səˋspɛnd | v. | 暫時停止 |
| headquarters | ˋhɛdˋkwɔrtɚs | n. | 總部 |
| request | rɪˋkwɛst | n. | 要求 |
| hardware | ˋhard͵wɛr | n. | 硬體 |

**Word Bank**

# Reading—Google

 MP3 008

Which search engine you use the most in your life? Do you know the meaning of "Google"? Google Inc. is an American multinational technology company. It is not so much a company that invents one product as a company that invents anything relating to the Internet. No matter if you agree with this saying or not, this company has a great **influence** on your daily life. You directly or indirectly use their service every day. Setting the goal of making the world's information universally **accessible** and useful, Google did make it and went much further. Starting from its core search engine, Google also offers email service—Gmail, a cloud storage service— Google drive, and a Web **browser**—Google Chrome. The Google self-driving car is also being invented. The scheduled release time is 2020.

## The original form of Google and its start

Though Google's service is **comprehensive** nowadays, their search engine was invented only for the purpose of research in the first place. The story begins with the time Sergey Brin and Larry Page, the founders, met each other at the **orientation** for new students at Stanford University. They became close friends after having a **disagreement** on most subjects. To get the data for the paper they co-authored, Brin and Page created a search engine that listed results according

自然科學和科技 1

青少年生活 2

世界文化和歷史 3

現代發明 4

to the popularity of the pages. That is the basic form of Google search. They named it "Google" after the mathematical term "googol" which means large numbers. This name reflects their mission to organize the huge amount of information on the Internet.

**The development of Google**

Google became a large enterprise within a short time. Noticing their searching engine becoming more and more popular, Brin and Page decided to **suspend** their studies and founded a company named of "Google" in 1998 in their friend's garage to carry forward the core value of their search engine. Soon, an initial public offering was offered for the company in 2004. There were about 20 million shares available at the price of $85 per share. In the same year, they moved to their new **headquarters** which is named Googleplex to Mountain View, California.

According to the statics in 2009, Google's search engine processed over one billion search **requests.** There were 24 petabytes of data generated by users each day. Google.com has been the most visited website in the world for years. By January 2014, Google's market capitalization had grown to $397 billion. Except for the development of software, Google put much effort into the invention of **hardware** like Google glasses.

# Multiple Choices 小知識選選看

❶ Why Brin and Page name their search engine "Google"?

(A) to reflect their goal to attract more users

(B) to reflect their ambition to become a big business

(C) to reflect their mission to organize information on the Internet

❷ When did Google firstly provide their shares to investors?

(A) in 2004

(B) in 2009

(C) in 2014

❸ Which of the following is the service provided by Google?

(A) Chrome

(B) Gmail

(C) all of the above

自然科學和科技 1

青少年生活 2

世界文化和歷史 3

現代發明 4

## ▶▶ 文章中譯

你每天最常使用哪種搜尋引擎呢？你知道"Google"這個詞的意思嗎？谷歌是美國的跨國科技公司。與其說谷歌發明了一項產品，倒不如說該公司發明了所有與網路有關的產品。無論你同不同意以上的言論，谷歌影響你的生活大小事，你每天都會直接或間接使用其服務。以整合全球資訊，使人人皆能使用與從中獲益為目標，谷歌不僅達到了目標且還更前進了一步。始自核心的搜尋引擎，谷歌現在更提供電子郵件服務 Gmail、雲端儲存服務 Google drive 以及網頁瀏覽器 Google Chrome。谷歌自動駕駛車輛也已開發多年，預計於 2020 年上市。

### 谷歌的最初樣貌與起源

雖然今日谷歌的服務已趨全面，但其搜尋引擎一開始僅為研究之用。發明的過程要從兩位創辦人謝爾蓋•布林與賴利•佩奇在史丹佛大學的新生訓練上認識說起。兩人從一開始的處處意見不合，到後來變成親密好友。為了取得兩人合著的論文所需的數據，他們發明了一個根據瀏覽次數排序網頁的搜尋引擎，而這就是谷歌搜尋的最初形態。布林與佩奇將此搜尋引擎命名為「谷歌」，其概念取自於數學上用來表達極大數字的「天文數字」一詞，這個名稱同時也反映了他們想將網際網路上巨大的資料量加以組織規劃的雄心壯志。

### 谷歌的發展

谷歌在短時間內就成為一間大企業。由於這個程式大受歡迎，布林與佩奇於 1998 年時決定休學，在朋友家的車庫以「谷歌」為名創立公司，以發揚其搜尋引擎的核心價值。很快地，谷歌於 2004 年首次公開上市，以每股 85 美金的金額提供近 2000 萬股給投資者。同年，谷歌公司也搬進他們位在加州山景城名為 Googleplex 的新總部。

　　根據 2009 年的統計資料，谷歌的搜尋引擎於該年一共處理超過 10 億個搜尋請求，每天用戶所產生的資料量更高達 24PB。多年來 Google.com 都是全球造訪量最大的網站。至 2014 年 1 月為止，谷歌的市值已增長至 3970 億美金。除了軟體上的發展，Google 在硬體上也投入很多心血研發像是 Google 眼鏡這類的產品。

## ▶ 選擇題中譯

❶ 為何布林與佩奇要將他們的搜尋引擎命名為「谷歌」？

(A) 表達他們要吸引更多用戶的目標

(B) 展現他們要成為大企業的野心

(C) 反映他們志在整合網路上的資訊

❷ 谷歌的股票於何時首次公開上市？

(A) 2004 年

(B) 2009 年

(C) 2014 年

❸ 谷歌提供以下哪些服務？

(A) Chrome 瀏覽器

(B) Gmail

(C) 以上皆是

選擇題答案：1.C　2.A　3.C

## Word Bank Youtube

| 字彙 | 音標 | 詞性 | 中譯 |
|---|---|---|---|
| hint | hɪnt | n. | 提示 |
| prioritize | praɪˋɔrəˌtaɪz | v. | 列為優先處理事項 |
| expertise | ˌɛkspɚˋtiz | n. | 專業知識 |
| matter | ˋmætɚ | v. | 要緊 |
| playlist | ˋplelɪst | n. | 播放清單 |
| affinity | əˋfɪnətɪ | n. | 吸引力 |
| engage | ɪnˋgedʒ | v. | 投入 |
| prompt | prɑmpt | adj. | 即時的 |
| feedback | ˋfidˌbæk | n. | 回饋 |
| annotation | ˌænoˋteʃən | n. | 註解 |

**Word Bank**

**Reading-The 10 Must Dos When You Start to Build Youtube Channel**

 MP3 009

In the information explosion era, building a Youtube Channel with abundant content sound like a tough task for a small business or organization. In fact, it is not that difficult if you review the resources you have first. Then, you can take a look at the ten **hints** which help you get a good start below.

### 1st hint – Set a goal for your channel

The first hint is setting up your goal. This step is **prioritized** for a reason. Once you set the goal, you can decide the type of videos you need to upload as well as the audience you would like to target. The second hint goes to creating your channel. This step will begin with a Google account application. When you have the account, you can log in in Youtube. Then, upload your company logo if you have one. If not, put an image that **expertise**. Thirdly, write an introduction with the link of the company website to help the audience know you more. Lastly, some artwork will make your channel look unique.

### The most important thing for Youtube – video making

The third hint is about video making. In this step, equipment isn't the key. Attitude **matters** more. Just have fun when you make a video, then your audience will have fun when watching it. The fourth hint is about creating **playlists** for your videos. When several videos have been shot, you have to group them together into a playlist. Then, give the playlist an eye-catching name. By doing so, your video can be found more easily in a Google search result.

Now we arrive on the halfway. In this step, you should make good use of other social networks such as Instagram and Twitter. With Youtube along, the **affinity** category of your videos is limited. Share your content on as many online media sites as you can. Here goes the sixth step. In this step, you have to review how the audience **engages** with your videos. In the best situation, the audience watches the content from beginning to the end. If they turn it off through halfway, you need to find the reason why and make some improvements.

## 8 and 9 Step – Keep the audience and use annotation

The seventh step is to think about how to keep the audience. Since the audience may have some questions or comments after watching your video, **prompt** and clear response help them learn more about your company. The eighth step is about the connection to Google plus. In the second step, you create a Google account. Therefore, you shouldn't forget its built-in social network. Link the two networks, and then you won't miss any **feedback**.

The ninth step is the use of **annotation**. This function can help promote your videos in a series. Once you put annotations on one of your videos, the audience has the opportunity to the watch the rest with a click. Lastly, verify your website periodically. Though it sounds boring and annoying, this step keeps your website running smoothly all the time.

## Multiple Choices 小知識選選看

❶ When making a video for your Youtube channel, what matters the most?

(A) your equipment

(B) your attitude

(C) your budget

❷ What's the function of annotation?

(A) To recommend other videos to the audience

(B) To generate data for analysis

(C) To review the audience's feedback

❸ Why you have to verify your Youtube Channel periodically?

(A) to get the feedback from the audience

(B) to ensure the contents go well

(C) to minimize the cost.

1 自然科學和科技

2 青少年生活

3 世界文化和歷史

4 現代發明

## ▶▶ 文章中譯

在資訊爆炸時代，建立有豐富內容的 Youtube 頻道對小公司或小機構來說似乎是件苦差事。事實上，如果先檢視手邊有哪些資源，做起來就不會這麼困難了。接著，不妨參考以下十項能夠讓你有好開始的小訣竅。

### 訣竅一：為你的頻道訂下目標

第一個小訣竅就是設定你的目標，這個步驟會被視為優先事項是有原因的。一旦設定好目標，就能決定影片類型以及目標觀眾是誰。第二個小訣竅是創立自己的頻道，這個步驟從申請 Google 帳號開始，有了帳號以後就能登入 Youtube。再來如果你的公司有商標的話，記得要上傳。沒有的話，找一個能展現公司專業的圖像來代替。接著，寫篇介紹文並於其中附上公司網站連結，好讓觀眾更認識你們公司。最後，做些美工能讓你的頻道看起來別具特色。

### Youtube 頻道最重要的元素：製作影片

第三個步驟是製作影片。在這個階段，用哪種器材來拍片並不是重點，更重要的是態度。拍片的時候要開心，這樣觀眾看你的影片時才會開心。第四個小訣竅是建立影片播放清單。當你拍攝了許多部影片後，必需將它們匯整起來並建立清單。然後替清單取個吸睛的名稱，這樣做可以讓你的影片更容易顯示在 Google 搜尋結果中。現在我們已經完成一半的步驟了。第五項是要善用其他社群網站，例如 Instagram 或是 Twitter。只靠 Youtube，觸及率很有限。你需要盡可能將影片分享至各大線上媒體。再來是第六步，這個步驟是檢視觀眾花多少時間看你的影片。在最好的情況下，他們有把影片從頭到尾看完。但如果他們中途就關閉影片，你就需要找出原因並加以改善。

### 訣竅八與九：留住觀眾與善用註解

第七點是思考如何留住觀眾。觀眾看完影片可能會提問或是留下評語，快速與清楚地給予回應能讓他們對你的公司更加了解。第八點是連結 **Google** plus。在步驟二時你創立了 **Google** 帳號，所以可別忘了使用它內建的社群媒體 **Google** plus。串聯 Youtube 與 **Google** plus，這樣你就不會遺漏任何觀眾回饋。

　　第九點是使用註解。這項功能可以幫助你一口氣推薦多部影片。只要將註解放在任何一部影片上，觀眾就有機會點擊觀賞其他影片。最後一個步驟是定期進行網站驗證。雖然這聽起來無聊且有些惱人，但這能確保網站隨時都運作順暢。

## ▶ 選擇題中譯

❶ 替自己的 Youtube 頻道拍攝影片時，最重要的是？

(A) 你的設備

(B) 你的態度

(C) 你的預算

❷ 註解的功用是？

(A) 向觀眾推薦其他影片

(B) 產生分析時所需的數據

(C) 檢視觀眾的回饋

❸ 為何要定期驗證自己的 Youtube 頻道？

(A) 從觀眾那得到回饋

(B) 確保內容運作順暢

(C) 將成本降到最低

選擇題答案：1.B　2.A　3.B

 **Word Bank Youtube**

| 字彙 | 音標 | 詞性 | 中譯 |
|---|---|---|---|
| hopeful | `hopfəl | n. | 希望獲得成功的人 |
| mecca | `mɛkə | n. | 熱門地點、聖地 |
| miniature | `mɪnɪətʃə | n. | 縮影 |
| subscriber | səb`skraɪbə | n. | 訂閱者 |
| exclusive | ɪk`sklusɪv | adj. | 獨家的 |
| springboard | `sprɪŋˌbord | n. | 跳板 |
| celebrity | sɪ`lɛbrətɪ | n. | 名人 |
| sponsorship | `spɑnsəˌʃɪp | n. | 贊助 |
| financial | faɪ`nænʃəl | adj. | 經濟的 |
| inevitable | ɪn`ɛvətəb! | adj. | 無可避免的 |

Word Bank

## Reading-How to Make Money by Being A Youtuber

MP3 010

For many generations of **hopefuls**, staying in LA to find a role in a film or TV program is their top choice. But there is a new kind of Hollywood named "Youtube" and Joey Ahern is one of many experiencing such change. He moved from south Florida to LA in 2014 for the reason that LA is the **mecca** for social media stars. Staying here can help him make more money and gain more followers. Now Ahern's Channel has hundreds of thousands of subscribers, and his story is the **miniature** of the development history of Youtubers.

**"Youtuber" as a career**

Youtubers refer to those who make "youtubing" their career. Top Youtubers, those with at least 3 million **subscribers**, enjoy not only fame but also wealth. Take PewDiePie for example, he earned at least $12 million in 2015 and fans recognize him easily if he shows up in a public place. Besides, Youtube invites famous creators like him to its **exclusive** party and provide extra resources. If a Youtuber becomes really well-known, big brands are definitely willing to invest money in his or her channel.

**The World of being a big Youtuber**

Being a Youtuber is easy but being a big Youtuber is super difficult nowadays as more and more people view this

1 自然科學和科技

2 青少年生活

3 世界文化和歷史

4 現代發明

as a platform the **springboard** for becoming a **celebrity**. With a Google account and a webcam, you can have your own channel. And this is the first intention this platform for why this platform was invented invented. But when gaining some fans, you have to worry about many things. Take another Youtuber, Hannah Hoffman, as an example, she earns less than the minimum wage from her channel. Therefore, getting brand **sponsorship** is crucial. The advertisements that run before videos are the most important **financial** support for Youtubers. When earning money, the pressure of generating more and more competition follows.

Since a Youtuber may run more than one channel, using Youtube's built-in analytics is **inevitable**. This program improves their channel and provides comprehensive statics but it is not free. Take Ahern as an example again, his analytics share 10 percent of the profit of the channel.

## Multiple Choices 小知識選選看

❶ What is the definition of a Youtuber?
(A) A person who likes to watch videos on Youtube
(B) A person view uploading videos to Youtube as a career
(B) A person who invests money in Youtube channels

❷ Why Youtubers need Youtube's built-in analysis software?
(A) They may rum more than one channel
(B) They need to know audiences' feedback
(C) all of the above

❸ What is the main financial support for Youtubers?
(A) Brand sponsorship
(B) The video itself
(C) Youtubers' own capital

▶▶ **文章中譯**

對有星夢的人來說，待在洛杉磯尋找一個電影或電視節目的演出機會絕對是首選。但現在有種全新型態的好萊塢—Youtube，而喬伊艾亨就是歷經此轉變的一員。2014 年時他從南佛羅里達搬到洛杉磯，理由是洛杉磯是社群媒體明星的聖地，待在此地可以讓他賺更多錢，並擁有更多追隨者。今日艾亨的頻道有數十萬的訂閱者，而他的故事正是 Youtuber 發展史的縮影。

## 以 Youtuber 做為職業

Youtuber 指的是以上傳影片至 Youtube 為業的一群人。頂尖的 Youtuber 至少都有三百萬的訂閱者，且名利雙收。以 PewDiePie 為例，他 2015 年至少賺了 1200 萬美金，且當他出現在公共場合時，粉絲可以輕易認出他。此外 Youtube 公司也會邀請像他這樣的知名創作者參加獨家派對，並提供額外資源。如果一個 Youtuber 真的紅到如日中天，大品牌絕對願意投資其頻道。

## 知名 Youtuber 的世界

要當 Youtuber 很簡單，但要出類拔萃非常困難，因為今日有越來越多人視這個平台為出名的跳板。一個 Google 帳號和一架網路攝影機在手，你就可以創立自己的頻道，而這也是 Youtube 成立的初衷。但當你累積到一定粉絲數後，就得擔心很多事情了。舉另一位 Youtuber 漢娜•霍夫曼為例，她從自己頻道賺到的錢比最低薪資還少，因此，獲得企業贊助十分重要。對 Youtuber 來說，影片播放前的廣告是他們最重要的收入來源。當 Youtuber 真的賺到點錢，如何賺更多以及如何面對激烈競爭的壓力也會接踵而至。

由於 Youtuber 可能同時經營多個頻道，使用平台內建的分析軟體看來勢在必行。這個軟體可以提升頻道品質、給予完整統計數據,但它不是免費的。再以艾亨為例,他頻道的利潤有百分之十是用來支付此軟體的費用。

## ▶ 選擇題中譯

❶ Youtuber 的定義是?

(A) 喜歡在 Youtube 上觀賞影片的人

(B) 以上傳影片至 Youtube 為業的人

(C) 投資 Youtube 頻道的人

❷ 為何 Youtuber 需要使用 Youtube 內建的分析軟體?

(A) 他們可能不只經營一個頻道

(B) 他們需要了解觀眾給予哪些回饋

(C) 以上皆是

❸ Youtuber 最主要的經濟來源是?

(A) 品牌贊助

(B) 影片本身

(C) Youtuber 自己的資金

選擇題答案:1.B 2.A 3.A

# 1-11 Automobiles
## 汽車

 **Word Bank 汽車**

| 字彙 | 音標 | 詞性 | 中譯 |
|------|------|------|------|
| engine | `ɛndʒɪn | n. | 引擎 |
| wheel | hwil | n. | 輪子 |
| history | `hɪstərɪ | n. | 歷史 |
| trace | tres | v. | 追溯 |
| gasoline | `gæsə͵lin | n. | 汽油 |
| apply | ə`plaɪ | v. | 應用 |
| traffic | `træfɪk | n. | 交通 |
| industry | `ɪndəstrɪ | n. | 產業 |
| travel | `trævl̩ | v. | 旅行、移動 |
| convenient | kən`vinjənt | adj. | 便利的 |

Word Bank

# Reading–Automobile

 MP3 011

Around 165,000 cars are produced every day. Cars are very important because they provide easy transportation or simply because cars amaze people. Are you able to name the person who invented the car? The answer to that question is "no one". No one single person invented the car.

## A lot of people contributed to the invention of cars

The average car has 30,000 parts. Car parts like **engine**s, **wheel**s, windshield or windshield wipers were all created by different people throughout **history**. The history of cars can probably be **trace**d back to the use of animals to carry things and creation of wheels. After that, more people became devoted to perfecting what would be needed later to make an automobile. Toward the end of the Middle Ages, inventors like Leonardo da Vinci drew sketches of automobiles that did not require animals before steam cars came along. However, the modern car did not show up until around 1885.

German engineer, Karl Benz, with the help from his wife, successfully built the first **gasoline**-powered automobile. The automobile created by Benz had three wheels and had a new type of engine built inside, which made the car similar to modern cars. The invention is considered the world's first

1 自然科學和科技

2 青少年生活

3 世界文化和歷史

4 現代發明

cars. In America, Henry Ford also built his own gasoline-powered automobile. Based on the ideas of the people before him, Ford **applied** assembly line techniques in his factory and was able to mass-produce cars, making them more affordable for people. Cars started to significantly change how people live around the world. Roads were rebuilt and new rules for **traffic** were set.

### The automotive industry in the United States

The automotive **industry**, especially in the United States, was thriving at the time. The U.S. dominated the global car market. Unfortunately, the Great Depression in the U.S. in the 1930s struck the industry hard. Even though economically, times were tough, more developments within the industry were made. The industry focused more on providing more quality mechanical traits. Almost all of the mechanical technology seen in today's cars had been invented by this time. The automotive industry boomed until the oil crisis of 1973 and the rapid growth of Asian manufacturers. Japan took over the market and became the leader of the automobile market. Not long after, in 2009, China rose and became the world's leading car manufacturer.

Automobiles are one of the most important inventions in the 20th century and they have made **travel**ing very **convenient**. Automotive engineers and car manufacturers have never stopped improving car technology. They also develop cars with self-parking capabilities or self-driving cars that will not need drivers. Self-driving cars might be difficult to imagine when the industry started booming. Now we can already see buses or taxis without human drivers that take people to places and also self-driving trucks that deliver products to customers.

## Multiple Choices 小知識選選看

_____ ❶ Which of the following is NOT an example of the progress of car technology?
(A) Seatbelts were invented to keep drivers safe.
(B) A car was designed in a way that it could use more gasoline.
(C) Special cars with no drivers were developed to carry things.

_____ ❷ According to the article, which of the following is TRUE?
(A) Unlike other inventions, it is difficult to name one person that invented cars.
(B) The Great Depression stopped all developments in the car industry.

1 自然科學和科技

2 青少年生活

3 世界文化和歷史

4 現代發明

(C) The U.S. still dominates the automobile market nowadays.

## ▶▶ 文章中譯

每天汽車的總生產量大約是 16 萬 5 千台，車子對很多人來說非常重要，因為為他提供方便的運輸方式，也是因為車子讓他們感到驚艷。而你有辦法說出是誰發明汽車的嗎？答案是「沒人」，汽車並非單一個人所發明的。

### 汽車是由很多人貢獻心血而發明出來的

一台車平均有 3 萬個零件，像引擎、車輪、擋風玻璃或雨刷等車組零件，全是由歷史上不同人所創造的。車子的歷史應該可以追溯到使用動物來運載東西以及輪子的發明，在這之後，更多人投入，讓後來能用來製作汽車的物件更加完善。接近中世紀末，達文西等發明家畫出不需要動物拖拉的車子草圖，接著蒸汽車也出現了，但現代汽車直到大約 1885 年才出現。

德國工程師卡爾‧賓士，在太太的協助之下，成功建造了第一台汽油動力汽車；賓士建造的汽車是三輪的，並內建一種新的引擎，這讓這種車很接近現代汽車。這兩項發明被視為是世界最早問世的汽車。在美國，亨利‧福特也建造了自己的汽油動力汽車，而且在以前人的想法為基礎下，他將生產線的技術整合後應用在自己的工廠，並開始大量生產汽車，讓人們更負擔得起汽車。車子於是開始在世界各地大幅度地改變人們的生活，道路歷經重建，也設立了新的交通規則。

### 美國的汽車業

汽車工業在當時蓬勃發展，尤其在美國，美國主導了全球的汽車市場。可惜的是，1930 年代美國的經濟大恐慌重創了這個產業。雖然在經濟上情況很艱難，但於此期間這個產業卻有更多的發展，更加注重提供具備優良性能的機械組件，大部分現代汽車看得到的機械技術都是在這時候發明的。汽車產業繁榮發展，直到 1973 年的石油危機，以及亞洲製造商的迅速發展。日本接收了市場，並成為汽車市場的領導者。不久後，在 2009 年中國崛起，變成全球領先的汽車製造商。

　　汽車是 20 世紀最重要的發明之一，它讓移動與旅行變得更方便。汽車工程師和汽車製造商一直馬不停蹄地讓汽車科技變得更好，也發展出有自動停車功能的車子，或是不需要駕駛的自駕車。在汽車產業剛開始的時候可能很難想像自駕車這樣的發明，現在我們已經可以看到沒有真人駕駛的公車或計程車，接送人們到不同的地方，也能看到自駕卡車遞送商品給客戶。

## ▶▶ 選擇題中譯

**❶** 以下哪個選項不是一個汽車科技更進步的例子？

(A) 為了讓駕駛更安全而發明安全帶。

(B) 汽車被設計成需要消耗更多汽油。

(C) 發展出沒有駕駛的特殊汽車來承載東西。

- - - - - - - - - - - - - - - - - - - - - - - - - - - - - - - - - - - - - - - -

**❷** 根據這篇文章以下哪個選項是正確的？

(A) 不像其他的發明，很難說出哪個人單獨發明車子。

(C) 經濟大恐慌阻止了汽車產業的所有發展。

(C) 美國現在還是主導著汽車市場。

- - - - - - - - - - - - - - - - - - - - - - - - - - - - - - - - - - - - - - - -

選擇題答案：1.B　2.A

# 1-12 Airplanes
飛機

## Word Bank 飛機

| 字彙 | 音標 | 詞性 | 中譯 |
|---|---|---|---|
| abroad | ə`brɔd | *adv.* | 出國 |
| country | `kʌntrɪ | *n.* | 國家 |
| passenger | `pæsndʒɚ | *n.* | 乘客 |
| flight | flaɪt | *n.* | 飛行 |
| wing | wɪŋ | *n.* | 翅膀 |
| power | `pauɚ | *n.* | 動力 |
| interest | `ɪntərɪst | *n.* | 興趣 |
| aircraft | `ɛr͵kræft | *n.* | 飛行器、飛機 |
| pilot | `paɪlət | *n.* | 駕駛員 |
| distance | `dɪstəns | *n.* | 距離 |

**Word Bank**

# Reading—Airplane

 MP3 012

Traveling **abroad**, especially alone, is a growing trend. Going to another **country** quickly would not be possible if planes had never been invented. Since the first airplane flew in 1903, it has been over a hundred years. During this time, hundreds and thousands of **passenger**s have traveled by air.

**The human desire to fly**

Perhaps since the dawn of time, people have always had the desire to fly. Before the first plane was invented, a lot of people devoted their time and energy to understanding the science of **flight**. Leonardo Da Vinci tried to imitate how animals like birds or bats fly and designed flying machines. More than 300 years later, Englishman Sir George Cayley successfully built the first manned glider (滑翔機) that was not powered and did not attempt to use flapping **wing**s. Afterward, steam engines were used in aircraft to provide **power** for flight.

**The Wright brothers and their first aircraft**

The Wright brothers, Orville and Wilbur Wright, built and sold bicycles and had a great understanding of mechanics. They started to develop an **interest** in **aircraft** and spent years studying how to make a better-powered aircraft. The brothers made use of a lot of concepts from bicycle making and gradually built the first aircraft that could be called an "airplane" because it was heavier than air and it was manned and powered. The aircraft could also take off and land on its own power. The most important thing was that a **pilot** had the three-axis control that allowed a better control and could better prevent crashes.

Finally, in 1903, the Wright brothers were ready to test the first airplane with a man on aboard. Three days before the famous successful flight, the two tried to fly their plane for the first time, but it did not go well and they damaged the plane. Fortunately, they did not give up. On December 17th, they gave it a second try and the flight lasted only 12 seconds. However, it was this 12-second flight that completely changed history. Even to this day, planes and pilots still use the skills and control system that was developed by the Wright brothers.

Right after the successful flight, the Wright brothers continued to improve their airplanes. Their planes inspired many engineers and inventors from around the world and led to many improvements and developments that gave birth to the airplanes we see today. The jet engine that enabled airplanes to fly faster and higher as well as pressurized cabins make it possible for planes with passengers to fly at a high altitude. It can be said that the 1930s were the most important period in aviation history (航空史). Thanks to airplanes, the

**distance** between two countries has been significantly shortened, and making travel between different countries becomes much easier.

## Multiple Choices 小知識選選看

❶ What is one of the reasons that made the Wright brothers' aircraft can be regarded as the first airplane?

(A) It could fly for a long time.

(B) It used flapping wings to fly.

(C) It was powered and had three-axis control.

❷ Which of the following is TRUE?

(A) Steam engines were used in airplanes at one point.

(B) The Wright brothers made the first successful plane by studying how birds fly.

(C) It is estimated that fewer people will travel by plane.

　　獨自一人出國旅行是個日益成長的趨勢，而如果飛機沒有被發明，那麼快速去到另一個國家是不可能發生的事。自從第一架飛機在 1903 年起飛後，到現在已經過了超過一百年，在這段時間，有成千上萬的乘客搭乘飛機旅遊，

## 人類對飛翔的渴望

　　可能自古以來，人類就一直有想要飛翔的慾望。在第一架飛機發明之前，很多人都投入時間與精力，試著想了解飛行的科學原理。李奧納多・達文西試著要模仿鳥兒或蝙蝠等動物飛行的方式，並設計飛行機器。逾三百多年之後，英國人喬治・凱利爵士成功建造第一部有載人的滑翔機，這部滑翔機沒有使用動力，也不嘗試使用拍打機翼的方式。在這之後，蒸汽引擎也被用在飛行器中，以提供飛行的動力。

## 萊特兄弟和他們的第一架飛機

　　奧維爾和威爾伯萊特兄弟製作並販售腳踏車，因此對機械學很了解。他們開始對飛行器感到興趣，花了好幾年研究怎麼做出更好、動力更強的飛行器。兩兄弟使用了許多製造腳踏車的概念，逐漸做出第一台可以被稱為「飛機」的飛行器，這台飛機比空氣重、可以載人也具備動力，還可以依靠自己的動力起飛跟降落，最重要的是，這台飛機有三軸控制系統，讓駕駛員可以更容易控制飛機，更可以避免墜機。

　　終於在 1903 年，萊特兄弟準備好讓一人上機，測試他們的第一部飛機了。在那有名的成功飛行的三天前，兩兄弟嘗試要第一次起飛，但並不順利，還損壞了飛機。好險他們並沒有放棄。就在 12 月 17 日這天，他們第二次嘗試，這次的飛行時間僅持續短短 12 秒，但這 12 秒卻徹底改變歷史，即使到今天，飛機與駕駛員仍在使用當初萊特兄弟發展出來的技術與控制系統。

　　在這趟成功的飛行之後，萊特兄弟繼續改良他們的飛機，而他們的飛機也激勵世界各地很多工程師與發明家，造就了無數的進步與發展，包含能讓飛機飛得更快、更高的噴射引擎，以及能讓有乘客的飛機飛在更高高度的壓力艙，誕生出我們現在看到的飛機，西元 1930 年可以說是航空歷史上最重要的一段時間。飛機的出現大大縮短了國家之間的距離，在不同國家間旅行對我們來說也變得更加容易。

## ▶▶ 選擇題中譯

❶ 萊特兄弟的飛行器可以被視為第一架飛機的原因之一為何？
　(A) 它可以飛很久。
　(B) 它使用拍打機翼的方式來飛行。
　(C) 它有動力和三軸控制系統。

- - - - - - - - - - - - - - - - - - - - - - - - - - - - - - - - - - - - - -

❷ 以下哪個選項是正確的？
　(A) 蒸汽引擎有一度被用在飛行器裡。
　(B) 萊特兄弟藉由研究鳥兒怎麼飛翔來做出第一架成功的飛機。
　(C) 根據預測，未來越來越少的人會使用飛機來移動。

- - - - - - - - - - - - - - - - - - - - - - - - - - - - - - - - - - - - - -

選擇題答案：1.C　2.A

1 自然科學和科技

2 青少年生活

3 世界文化和歷史

4 現代發明

# 1-13 Online Courses
## 線上課程

 **Word Bank 網路課程**

| 字彙 | 音標 | 詞性 | 中譯 |
|---|---|---|---|
| education | ɛdʒʊˋkeʃən | n. | 教育 |
| popular | ˋpɑpjələ | adj. | 受歡迎的 |
| distance | ˋdɪstəns | n. | 距離 |
| invite | ɪnˋvaɪt | v. | 邀請 |
| difference | ˋdɪfərəns | n. | 差異 |
| provide | prəˋvaɪd | v. | 提供 |
| knowledge | ˋnɑlɪdʒ | n. | 知識 |
| skill | ˋskɪl | n. | 技能 |
| discuss | dɪˋskʌs | v. | 討論 |
| traditional | trəˋdɪʃənl | adj. | 傳統的 |

Word Bank

## Reading—Online Courses

MP3 013

Online **education** is becoming so **popular** that even top universities like Harvard or Stanford offer many online courses to their students or even people outside of the schools. Online courses have changed a lot of people's lives because of all the benefits they bring. However, online courses may not be suitable for everyone.

**How Online Courses Got Started**

The earliest **distance** learning probably started from a teacher in England that **invite**d people to copy texts in shorthand and send the results to him for feedback. After the appearance of computers and the Internet, online learning was made possible. Sometimes, it is called "distance learning" and "online learning". In fact, there are slight **difference**s between distance learning and online learning. Distance learning implies that the teacher and the student are in different places. On the other hand, online learning can be applied in classrooms with teachers leading students. Here we will use "online learning" in a broader sense to include distance learning.

**The advantages and disadvantages of online learning**

There are many advantages to online learning. Online

classes **provide** chances to learn new **knowledge** and **skill**s in the comfort of your home at any time of the day. Even when you are in Taiwan, you can take classes offered by universities in Europe and America. Besides, most of the online classes allow you to be flexible and enter the classroom online whenever you want. It is best for adults who have very limited time. People who have a job or have children may not be able to attend classes on a fixed schedule. With online courses, they can study after they are off work or when their kids are sleeping. If something happens, they can skip a day and continue the next. Also, learning online can cost you less money. You do not have to pay as many fees to the school or buy as many books.

Being such a wonderful learning tool, online courses may not for everyone. There are some downsides that people overlook. First of all, although there are more ways now for students to **discuss** things with their teachers or classmates, the interaction may not be as effective as it is in **traditional** classrooms because people may not be able to see facial expressions or body language. Moreover, different from what most people think, much more effort needs to be put in when one is studying online.

With a lot of reading and listening and less interaction, some students may find it boring and would have a hard time finishing a course. Also, since online courses are normally flexible, it is easy for students to want to skip classes when they do not feel like studying. Therefore, online learning requires students to discipline themselves and have great time management skills.

## Multiple Choices 小知識選選看

❶ What is most likely the reason why someone chooses to take online courses?
(A) The person loves to interact with people and watch how people respond.
(B) The person, who has to work in the morning, wants to improve his or her speaking skills.
(C) The person wants to learn new skills but he or she needs a teacher to discipline them.

❷ Which of the following statements best summarizes this article?
(A) Taking online courses is a great way to learn new knowledge and skills.
(B) Online education has its advantages and disadvantages and we should decide how we use it.

(C) Online learning is so wonderful that we should all do it.

## ▶ 文章中譯

　　線上教學越來越受歡迎，連哈佛、史丹佛等頂尖大學都為學生設立許多網路課程，甚至提供給校外的人。因為線上課程帶來的優點，它們改變了很多人的人生，但是線上課程可能未必適合每個人。

**線上課程的起源**

　　最早的遠距教學可能始於一位在英國的老師，他邀請大家速記抄寫文章，並寄給他批改。在電腦和網路的出現後，線上學習變得可行。有時人們稱之為「遠距教學」，或是「線上教學」，但其實遠距教學與線上教學有些許不同，例如：遠距教學意味著老師和學生是在不同的地方，線上教學則可應用在教室中，由老師帶領學生。在這裡我們會以較廣泛的意思來使用「線上教學」這個詞，涵蓋遠距教學的意思。

**線上教學的優點與缺點**

　　線上教學有許多優點。線上課程提供學習新知與新技術的機會，而且可以留在舒服的家裡，挑選自己想要上課的時間，即使你在台灣，也可以上歐洲和美國大學提供的課程。 此外，大部分的線上課程都很彈性，你可以選擇自己要的時間進入線上教室。這對時間有限的成人特別有幫助，有工作或有小孩的人可能無法在固定時間上課；有了線上課程，他們可以在下班時間或是當小孩在睡覺時開始上課，如果臨時有其他更重要的事需要處理，他們也可以跳過一天，隔天再繼續。而且，線上學習所需要的花費較少，你不需要付給學校那麼多費用，也不需要買那麼多書。

　　線上課程是個很棒的學習工具，但卻不一定適合每個人。線上課程有些大家常忽略的缺點。首先，雖然現在有越來越多的方法讓學生可以和老師或同學線上討論事情，但是線上的互動可能不如傳統教室的互動來得有效，因為人們無法判斷他人的臉部表情或肢體動作。此外，與大多數人所想的不同，線上學習需要投入更多的努力。因為需要大量閱讀或聆聽，互動也變少了，有些學生可能會覺得無聊，沒辦法完成一個課程，再加上線上課程通常都很彈性，學生很容易不想唸書的時候就不上課。所以線上學習時，學生必須督促好自己，並且要有很好的時間管理技巧。

▶▶ **選擇題中譯**

❶ 以下哪個選項最可能是一個人選擇上線上課程的原因？

(A) 這個人喜歡和人互動以及觀察人們怎麼回應

(B) 這個人早上必須工作，但想要增進自己的口說技巧

(C) 這個人想要學新技能，但需要一個老師來督促他

- - - - - - - - - - - - - - - - - - - - - - - - - - - - - - - - - - - - -

❷ 以下哪個描述最符合本文大意？

(A) 選修線上課程是個學習新知識與技能的好方法。

(B) 線上教育有優點也有缺點，我們應該決定如何使用它。

(C) 線上學習非常棒，我們都應該使用它。

- - - - - - - - - - - - - - - - - - - - - - - - - - - - - - - - - - - - -

選擇題答案：1.B　2.B

# 1-14 Nuclear Power
## 核能發電

 **Word Bank 核能發電**

| 字彙 | 音標 | 詞性 | 中譯 |
|---|---|---|---|
| energy | `ɛnɚdʒɪ | n. | 能量 |
| opinion | ə`pɪnjən | n. | 意見 |
| electricity | ilɛk`trɪsətɪ | n. | 電 |
| weapon | `wɛpən | n. | 武器 |
| accident | `æksədənt | n. | 事故 |
| waste | west | n. | 廢棄物 |
| disadvantage | ˌdɪsəd`væntɪdʒ | n. | 不利條件、缺點 |
| benefit | `bɛnəfit | n. | 優勢 |
| source | sors | n. | 來源 |
| alternative | ɔl`tɝnətɪv | n. | 可替代的東西或辦法 |

**Word Bank**

# Reading—Nuclear Power

 MP3 014

On March 11th, 2011, an earthquake with a the magnitude of nine in northeastern Japan caused a very powerful tsunami. The earthquake and the tsunami damaged a nuclear power plant, which became the second worst nuclear accident in history. After the disaster, people's fear of nuclear power was intensified, which again generated heated worldwide debate about nuclear **energy**. People around the world have different **opinion**s on this issue.

**What exactly is nuclear energy?**

Nuclear energy is energy that is generated from nuclear reactions. The energy is then used to produce **electricity** in nuclear power plants in the same way other kinds of power plants generate electricity. In the 19th century, scientists made great progress in physics and found that fission reactions create a lot of energy. They were also able to achieve controlled nuclear chain reactions. This was right before World War II and these discoveries were mainly used in the making of atomic **weapon**s. Later, scientists focused on peaceful applications of nuclear technology such as generating electricity. Because of the use of atomic bombs in the Second World War and the threat of nuclear wars that is still present today, people cannot help but be reminded of weapons whenever nuclear power is mentioned.

## The waste of nuclear energy and nuclear radiation accidents

What worries people the most about nuclear power plants is the possibility of nuclear radiation **accident**s. We have seen some serious accidents such as the Chernobyl (車諾比) disaster and the Fukushima Daiichi (福島) nuclear disaster, and the economic and environmental damage they have caused, not to mention the effect they have on human health. What is more troubling about nuclear power plants is the **waste**. The radioactive waste, especially high-level waste, needs to be stored safely to avoid the release of deadly radiation. However, we only have temporary methods to store this waste. This threats along with other problems, encourages people and governments to reject the use of nuclear energy and turn to renewable energy.

## The benefits of nuclear energy

Despite the **disadvantage**s, some people would argue that the **benefit**s of nuclear energy outweigh the risks. Unlike most renewables, nuclear energy is predictable and reliable. Nuclear power plants can produce electricity around the clock without depending on the weather. Solar or wind power sometimes does not generate enough power, while at other times creates a lot more electricity than can be stored. Nuclear energy is also efficient, using only small amounts of uranium (鈾) and losing very little energy in the process. In addition, it is relatively more eco-friendly, emitting much less greenhouse gas than other traditional or renewable power **sources**. Even though radioactive waste has many issues waiting to be solved, scientists are looking at a possible technology to reuse the high-level waste. As we can no longer rely on fossil fuels, finding **alternative** energy sources is crucial. However, up to today, the world has still not reached a consensus on using nuclear energy as an alternative.

## Multiple Choices 小知識選選看

❶ Why do people think of weapons when they hear nuclear energy?

(A) Nuclear power plants look like weapons.

(B) People who work in nuclear power plants are required to carry weapons.

(C) People have used nuclear energy to build atomic bombs.

❷ According to the article, which of the following is NOT an advantage of nuclear energy?

(A) Nuclear energy is not affected by the weather.

(B) Using nuclear energy frees us from worrying about our health.

(C) We can control the amount of electricity

1 自然科學和科技

2 青少年生活

3 世界文化和歷史

4 現代發明

produced.

## ▶ 文章中譯

在 2011 年 3 月 11 日，一場規模九級的大地震襲擊日本東北方，並造成威力強大的海嘯。地震與海嘯破壞了核能電廠，造成歷史上第二嚴重的核子事故。這場災難之後，人們對核能的恐懼加深了，再度引起世界各地關於核能的激烈討論。世界各地的人們針對這個議題都有不同的意見，要得到一個結論並不容易。

**什麼是核能？**

核能就是由核反應產生的能量，這種能量又在核電廠裡被用來發電，發電方式就和其他種類的發電廠相同。在 19 世紀時，科學家在物理的領域有很大的進展，也發現核分裂可以產生巨大的能量，科學家後來還成功地控制核連鎖反應。這一切都在第二次世界大戰之前，所以這些發現都被用在製作核武器，後來科學家則專注在核科技的和平運用，如用來發電。因為二次大戰使用的原子彈，再加上現今還是存在的核武戰爭的威脅，談到核能時人們總不禁想到武器。

**核廢料和核輻射事故**

說到核能電廠，人們最擔心的就是核輻射事故發生的可能。我們已經經歷過車諾比核電事故以及福島第一核電廠事故等嚴重的核能災害，也看到它們在經濟和環境上造成的損害，更別提對人類健康的影響。更令人憂心的是核電廠的核廢料，有放射性的核廢料，尤其是高階放射性廢料，必須要被安全的永久儲存，以避免致命的放射線外露，然而，目前我們只有核廢料暫時的儲存方式。這樣的威脅加上其他的問題刺激許多民眾與政府拒絕使用核能，改為使用再生能源。

**核能發電的優點**

雖然核能有以上缺點，也有許多人會說核能的優點遠超過使用核能的風險。不像大部分的再生能源，核能發電可預期、也較可靠。核能電廠能全年發電，不需依靠天氣，太陽能或風力發電則會有產出電量不足的時候或是製造出的電量遠超過儲存機制能負荷的上限。核能發電也較有效率，使用的鈾很少，而且發電過程中浪費的能量也很少。此外，核能發電相較之下對環境也比較友善，因為它比其他傳統或再生能源釋放的溫室氣體少很多。雖然核廢料還是一個需要處理的問題，科學家正在研究可以重複利用高階核廢料的可行性。因為我們已經不能依賴化石燃料，找到替代能源是很重要的，不過現今世界各地的人對於以核能當作替代能源還沒有得到共識。

## ▶▶ 選擇題中譯

❶ 人們為什麼一聽到核能就想到武器？

(A) 核電廠看起來像武器。

(B) 在核電廠工作的人必須要攜帶武器。

(C) 人們曾經使用核能製造原子彈。

⋯⋯⋯⋯⋯⋯⋯⋯⋯⋯⋯⋯⋯⋯⋯⋯⋯⋯⋯⋯⋯⋯⋯⋯⋯⋯⋯⋯⋯⋯⋯

❷ 根據這篇文章，以下哪個選項不是核能的優點？

(A) 核能不會受到天氣的影響。

(B) 使用核能，我們就不用擔心我們的健康。

(C) 我們可以控制要生產多少電。

⋯⋯⋯⋯⋯⋯⋯⋯⋯⋯⋯⋯⋯⋯⋯⋯⋯⋯⋯⋯⋯⋯⋯⋯⋯⋯⋯⋯⋯⋯⋯

選擇題答案：1.C　2.B

1 自然科學和科技

2 青少年生活

3 世界文化和歷史

4 現代發明

# Part 2 青少年生活

　　學校是青少年們生活的一大重心，但青春期也是孩子成長的一個關鍵時期，除了需要面臨成長中身體的變化，也需要面對課業和同儕的壓力。特別是現代的孩子生於網路世代，一個擁有更多選擇的世代，一個快速變遷的世代。本篇共六個單元，特別收錄一些專屬青少年的困擾，青少年戀愛、網路霸凌和尋找夢想，希望幫助成長中的孩子解開生活中不敢開口的青春心事。

## Word Bank

| 字彙 | 音標 | 詞性 | 中譯 |
| --- | --- | --- | --- |
| hazard | ˋhæzɚd | n. | 危害 |
| adolescence | æd!ˋɛsns | n. | 青春期 |
| toxic | ˋtɑksɪk | adj. | 有毒的，中毒的 |
| cerebellum | ͵sɛrəˋbɛləm | n. | 小腦 |
| impulse | ˋɪmpʌls | n. | 衝動 |
| blackout | ˋblæk͵aʊt | n. | 斷片 |
| unbeknownst | ˋʌnbɪˋnonst | adv. | 不知情地 |
| parallel | ˋpærə͵lɛl | adj. | 平行的 |
| neurotoxin | ͵njʊroˋtɑksɪn | n. | 神經毒素 |

Word Bank

**Reading-The Unique Risks of Smoking and Alcohol for Teens**

 MP3 015

We all know that drinking and smoking will harm our body but we may not know they may pose more unique **hazards** for teenagers than the usual health and addiction risks. Although a teenager's brain is about the same size as an adult's, it is qualitatively (質地上地) quite different because it's not yet fully formed. Throughout **adolescence**, three major brain regions, the frontal lobes (額葉), the hippocampus (海馬迴), and the **cerebellum**, undergo the major developments of intricate (錯綜複雜的) branches and the making of new connections. Now, new evidences have suggested that alcohol and cigarettes may have an especially damaging effect on those developing brains.

**Alcohol is toxic to youth's frontal lobes – their decision making and impulse control.**

According to the research of the neuroscientist (神經學家) Aaron White from Duke University, the younger we are, the more sensitive those areas of the brain mentioned above are to alcohol. Take the frontal lobe as an example, it is in charge of decision making and **impulse** control. However, alcohol is **toxic** to it. When teenagers drink, they tend to make bad decisions and have poor emotion control. White also believes that there may be no safe level of alcohol for teenagers, so the way they drink makes the situation even worse.

Teenagers drink infrequently, but when they drink, they drink a lot and chug it down very quickly. Therefore, the most common result is alcoholic (酒精的) **blackouts**; a person is fully awake but **unbeknownst** to to not all of his such as hippocampus are functioning. Researcher Ron Dahl, from the University of Pittsburgh, also says this indicated that the cerebellum is very late developing into late adolescence (青春期) and sensitive to alcohol.

## Nicotine affects teenagers' memories the most.

It's commonly believed by young people that the ill effects of smoking don't really start until you're in middle age. But the real situation is not quite like they think. From a study by research psychiatrist Leslie Jacobsen from Yale University's School of Medicine, we can tell that smoking affects teenagers' memories the most. In the test which checks verbal working memory, Jacobsen compares the performance of smokers and that of non-smokers. Regardless of how recently the smokers had smoked, they performed worse on the working memory task. The study also points out that **parallel** evidence from studies with animals show that nicotine (尼古丁) is a **neurotoxin** (神經毒素). That is, nicotine kills cells; specifically, in brain areas critical for learning and memory.

## Multiple Choices 小知識選選看

❶ What is the common drinking habit which teenagers have?

(A) They drinks infrequently

(B) They drink slowly

(C) They drink only small amount a time

❷ What dose blackout means here?

(A) The person who can see nothing temporarily after drinking

(B) The person is still awake but unbeknownst to some part of his or her brain isn't functioning after drinking

(C) The person who can do nothing but sleep after drinking

❸ According to this article, nicotine is _____.

(A) not harmful to teenagers' brain

(B) one kind of neurotoxin

(C) one kind of substance which can't affect our performance in memorizing things.

1 自然科學和科技

2 青少年生活

3 世界文化和歷史

4 現代發明

## ▶ 文章中譯

　　我們都知道喝酒與抽菸對身體不好，但我們可能不知道比起一般人，它們會對青少年造成更多健康上的危害，且更容易引發成癮問題。雖然青少年的大腦尺寸已與成人相差無幾，但在性質上仍天差地遠，因為青少年的大腦尚未發育完全。在整個青春期中，大腦中的三個主要區塊：額葉、海馬迴和小腦都在進行極重要的發展，產生錯綜複雜的分支以及新的連結。現在有新的證據指出酒精和香菸特別容易對這些發育中的大腦造成損傷。

## 酒精對年輕人做出決策和情緒控制的額葉是毒藥

　　根據杜克大學神經學家艾倫•懷特的研究，年紀越輕，上述大腦中的那些區塊就對酒精越敏感。以額葉為例，它掌管了決策制定與衝動控制，但酒精對它而言可以說是毒藥。一旦青少年有喝酒，就容易做出錯誤決定，情緒控管也會變差。艾倫也相信可能根本沒有所謂的青少年安全飲酒量；正因如此，青少年喝酒的方式常讓情況變得更糟。

　　青少年並不常喝酒，但一喝就喝很多而且喝得很快。因此，最常出現的結果就是斷片；也就是人是清醒的，但自己並不知道大腦某些部分，例如海馬迴沒有在運作。匹茲堡大學的研究人員隆•達爾也指出，小腦要到青春期後期才會開始發展，且對酒精十分敏感。

## 尼古丁影響年輕人的記憶力最劇

　　年輕人普遍相信抽菸所產生的不良影響要到中年才會發生，但實際情況可沒他們想的這麼好。根據耶魯大學醫學院精神學家萊斯里•雅各布森的研究，我們可以得出抽菸對於青少年的記憶影響最為巨大。在語言工作記憶的測試中，雅各布森比對了吸菸者與非吸菸者的表現。無論吸菸者是多久以前抽菸，其工作記憶總是較差。研究也指出從以動物為實驗對象研究的平行證據中，我們可得知尼古丁是一種神經毒素。換言之，尼古丁會殺死細胞，特別是大腦中那些對學習和記憶不可或缺的細胞。

## ▶▶ 選擇題中譯

❶ 青少年常見的飲酒習慣是？

　(A) 他們不常喝酒

　(B) 他們喝酒時喝很慢

　(C) 他們喝酒時一次只喝一點點

❷ 此處的斷片指的是？

　(A) 人在喝酒後暫時失去視力

　(B) 人在喝酒後仍保持清醒，但卻不知道大腦中有些部分並沒有在運作

　(C) 人在喝酒後什麼都不做就只能一直昏睡

❸ 根據此文章，尼古丁是 _____？

　(A) 對青少年大腦無害

　(B) 一種神經毒素

　(C) 一種無法影響記憶表現的物質

選擇題答案：1.A　2.B　3.B

# Bullying
## 2-2 霸凌—英國教育與技術部發行中小學反霸凌處理程序書

 **Word Bank 霸凌**

| 字彙 | 音標 | 詞性 | 中譯 |
|---|---|---|---|
| reference | `rɛfərəns | *n.* | 參考資料 |
| conduct | kən`dʌkt | *v.* | 施行 |
| individual | ˌɪndə`vɪdʒʊəl | *n.* | 個人 |
| depressed | dɪ`prɛst | *adj.* | 沮喪的 |
| attempt | ə`tɛmpt | *v.* | 試圖做… |
| principal | `prɪnsəpl | *n.* | 校長 |
| intervention | ˌɪntə`vɛnʃən | *n.* | 介入 |
| victim | `vɪktɪm | *n.* | 受害者 |
| self-esteem | ˌsɛlfəs`tim | *n.* | 自尊 |
| domestic | də`mɛstɪk | *adj.* | 家庭的 |

**Word Bank**

# Reading—Bullying

 MP3 016

Bullying happens all time in schools because children spend a significant portion of their time there and are in large social groups. It is a problem which should not be neglected. To prevent this problem from getting worse, the Department of Education and Skills published the Anti-Bullying Procedures for Primary and Post-Primary Schools for teachers as a **reference**.

According to the Department of Education and Skills' definition, bullying means unwanted negative verbal, psychological or physical behavior. It can be **conducted** by an **individual** or group against another person or persons and it is repeated over time. Due to the development of the Internet, placing an offensive or hurtful public message on a social media network is also regarded as bullying. Though the bullied are often afraid of speaking out, there are some signs of bullying. When one is bullied in school, he or she often becomes unconfident, **depressed**, and unable to concentrate. Soon, he or she may fear going to school. In extreme cases, they even **attempt** to suicide.

To stop bullying, two things should be done. One is an anti-bullying policy should be established in all schools. From

1　自然科學和科技

2　青少年生活

3　世界文化和歷史

4　現代發明

the **principal** to teachers, they need to know what to do step by step when bullying happens. And such information should be available on the school website. The other is adults' **intervention** and care for both those bullying and the bullied. When someone is bullied, you should take some time to win their trust. Then, they will tell you what happened. Since the bullied are the **victims**, we often neglect the fact that the bullying could be victims, too. Bullies are often the ones with low **self-esteem**. They may suffer from **domestic** violence, and then they treat their schoolmates the same way. Helping them to solve their problem could prevent new bullying behaviors from happening.

## Multiple Choices 小知識選選看

❶ Bullying could be conducted in the way of _____.
   (A) words
   (B) actions
   (C) all of above

❷ When one is bullied, he or she will become_____.
   (A) aggressive
   (B) unconfident
   (C) more concentrate on studies

❸ To stop bullying, adults should_____.
   (A) spend some time to win trust from the bullied
   (B) keep blaming the bullying
   (C) avoid setting SOP

## ▶▶ 文章中譯

因為學生待在學校的時間十分地長，加上學校本身就是一個大型的社會群體，因此校園霸凌事件屢見不鮮。這是個不該被忽略的問題，為了避免情況繼續惡化，英國的教育與技術部發行了中小學反霸凌處理程序書給老師們做參考。

依照教育與技術部的定義，霸凌指的是讓人厭惡的負面言語、心理或身體上的行為。霸凌可能是一對一、一對多或多對一、多對多，並且在一段時間內重複發生。由於網路的普及，在社群媒體上散布冒犯他人或具傷害性的公開訊息也被視為霸凌。當某人遭到霸凌時，他們通常沒有勇氣為自己發聲，但是我們仍然可以從一些蛛絲馬跡發現霸凌的徵兆。在學校遭受霸凌的孩子經常會變得沒有自信、沮喪且無法專心。很快地，他們會不敢去上學，在極端案例中被霸凌者甚至會想自殺。

若要停止霸凌，得做到兩點：一是所有學校都要明文規定反霸凌政策，從校長到老師都該清楚霸凌事件發生時該如何一步步處理。這些資料也必須在學校網站上找得到；另一點是大人對霸凌者與被霸凌者的介入處理與關懷。當發現有學生受到霸凌時，你得花點時間贏得對方的信任，然後他們就會告訴你事情的來龍去脈。由於被霸凌者是受害者，我們常忽略霸凌者本身也可能是受害者。霸凌者通常很自卑，他們在家可能被暴力相向，因此用相同方式對待學校同學，幫助他們可以防止新的霸凌事件再度發生。

## ▶▶ 選擇題中譯

❶ 霸凌可以透過_____的方式進行。

　(A) 言語

　(B) 行動

　(C) 以上皆是

. . . . . . . . . . . . . . . . . . . . . . . . . . . . . . . . . . . . . . . . . . . . . . . . . . . . . . .

❷ 當某人遭受霸凌，他或她會變得_____。

　(A) 具攻擊性

　(B) 缺乏信心

　(C) 更專心學習

. . . . . . . . . . . . . . . . . . . . . . . . . . . . . . . . . . . . . . . . . . . . . . . . . . . . . . .

❸ 為了停止霸凌，成人們應_____。

　(A) 花時間贏得被霸凌者的信任

　(B) 一直責備霸凌者

　(C) 避免建立標準作業

. . . . . . . . . . . . . . . . . . . . . . . . . . . . . . . . . . . . . . . . . . . . . . . . . . . . . . .

選擇題答案：1.C　2.B　3.A

1 自然科學和科技

2 青少年生活

3 世界文化和歷史

4 現代發明

# 2-3 Teenage Love
## 青少年的戀愛

 **Word Bank 戀愛**

| 字彙 | 音標 | 詞性 | 中譯 |
|---|---|---|---|
| teenager | `tinˌedʒɚ | *n.* | 青少年 |
| puberty | `pjubɚtɪ | *n.* | 青春期 |
| feeling | `filɪŋ | *n.* | 感覺 |
| confuse | kənˈfjuːz | *v.* | 使困惑 |
| embarrassed | ɪm`bærəst | *adj.* | 尷尬的 |
| understand | ˌʌndɚ`stænd | *v.* | 理解 |
| unconditional | ˌʌnkən`dɪʃənḷ | *adj.* | 無條件的 |
| dismiss | dɪs`mɪs | *v.* | 不考慮 |
| responsibility | rɪˌspɑnsə`bɪlətɪ | *n.* | 責任 |
| respect | rɪ`spɛkt | *v.* | 尊重 |

**Word Bank**

## Reading—Teenage Love

MP3 017

Over 400 years ago in 1595 AD, Shakespeare wrote Romeo and Juliet, a story that portrayed, among other things, the pure and strong love between two **teenager**s. The story has touched the hearts of many young people who have similar feelings or yearn to experience such feelings.

### The Love Feeling in Puberty

As a teenager, especially if you just entered **puberty**, it is easy to find yourself being attracted to your classmates or friends. You cannot stop thinking about this person and want to see him or her all the time. The romantic **feeling** can be so intense that it **confuse**s and scares you since you have never experienced something like it before. Very likely, you will have mixed feelings, hoping the person you are attracted to will notice you and wanting to run away because you are **embarrassed**. It is common for someone not to return your feelings. It will hurt but it does not mean you are not good enough or that there is something wrong with you. The feeling of attraction may all just be a crush (迷戀) and the feelings may quickly fade away. You do not have to fight such feelings because it is a good time for you to **understand** what it means to like someone and you will get to know yourself better.

**Talk to some adults about your feelings.**

The crush may also develop into love. The feelings you have for the person are much stronger and want to really get to know this person. Love is longer-lasting and rather **unconditional**. Most adults may **dismiss** your feeling of being in love with someone, but teenagers fall in love just like adults. However, you have to admit that teenagers are not as mature. At this stage of life, you are still trying to figure many things out. Most of the time, you may not know what to do. It really helps to have a sincere (真摯的) conversation with your parents, teachers, or adults that you trust, and talk about how you feel. If you do enter a relationship with someone, there will be many more problems to deal with than you can imagine. You may have to face jealousy, heartbreak or pressure. Ask for guidance from adults and be ready to follow some rules they set.

**Love is not just about the desire to be with the one you love.**

Love is not just about the desire to be with each other. Love and romantic relationships actually encompass many **responsibilities**. They require communication and teamwork. This is how the relationship can develop and grow. The most important thing is to **respect** each other and avoid being affected by peer pressure. Do not force people to change themselves for you and never allow your partner to force you to do anything you do not feel like doing.

## Multiple Choices 小知識選選看

_____ ❶ Which of the following is NOT true?

(A) It is natural for someone not to share the feelings you have for them.

(B) If your love is not returned, you should immediately examine yourself.

(C) You do not have to feel embarrassed about being attracted to your classmate.

_____ ❷ What does it mean to be really in love with someone?

(A) You have a very strong and lasting romantic feeling about someone.

(B) You think you like someone and then forget about it a week after.

(C) You want to control someone and get angry if they do not listen to you.

_____ ❸ Which of the following is what you do when you are confused about the feelings you have for someone?

(A) Act on all the feelings you have.

(B) Ignore the feelings and move on with your life.

(C) Discuss your feelings with an adult you can rely on.

1 自然科學和科技

2 青少年生活

3 世界文化和歷史

4 現代發明

超過 400 年前，在西元 1595 年，莎士比亞寫了《羅密歐與茱麗葉》，這個故事談到很多層面，其中更描述了兩個青少年之間單純且強烈的愛情。這故事觸動了許多年輕人的心，他們有著與主角類似的感受或是渴望能夠體驗這樣的情感。

## 青春期的戀愛感覺

身為青少年，尤其如果你剛進入青春期，你可能很容易就發現自己被同學或朋友吸引，你沒辦法停止想念這個人，隨時都想看到他或她。這種戀愛的感覺可能會強烈到讓你覺得很困惑且害怕，畢竟你從沒有經歷過這樣的感覺。你非常有可能會有交錯複雜的感覺，既希望你有興趣的那個人可以注意到你，但同時也因為尷尬而想要逃跑。對方如果無法回應你的感覺是很常見的，你會感到受傷，但這絕對不是因為你不夠好，或是有什麼問題。你被某人吸引的這種感覺或許只是短暫的迷戀，可能隨著時間很快就流逝。你並不需要抗拒這種感覺，因為透過這樣的經驗，你會了解喜歡一個人是什麼意思，也是更了解自己的好時機。

## 跟大人談談你的感覺

暗戀也可能發展成愛，這時你對某個人的感覺更加深刻，你真的想認識這個人。「愛」持續的時間更長久，而且可以說是毫無條件的，大部分的成人可能不會把你愛上某人的感覺當一回事，其實青少年就像成人一樣會墜入愛河。然而，你必須承認，青少年還沒有那麼成熟。在人生的這個階段，你有很多事情需要搞清楚，大部分的時候可能不知道該怎麼做。和你的父母、老師或你相信的成人進行真誠的對話，聊一聊你的感受可以給你許多幫助。如果你真的和某人開始交往了，還有更多超越你想像的問題在等待著你，你可能需要面對嫉妒、心碎或壓力，向成人尋求一些導引，並準備好遵守一些他們設下的規則吧！

### 愛不只是想與對方在一起的念頭

　　愛不只是想要和對方在一起。愛以及戀愛關係其實涵蓋了許多責任，必須要有溝通以及良好的合作，戀情才有辦法發展和成長，最重要的是彼此尊重，而且不要受到同儕壓力影響，不要強迫對方為了你而改變自己，也千萬不要允許你的伴侶強迫你去做任何你不想做的事情。

### ▶▶ 選擇題中譯

❶ 以下哪個選項不正確？
(A) 你喜歡別人，而對方不喜歡你是很正常的。
(B) 如果你付出的愛沒有得到回報，你應該馬上檢視自己哪裡做錯。
(C) 你如果被同學吸引，不需要覺得丟臉。

❷ 真的愛一個人是什麼意思？
(A) 你對一個人有很強烈且持久的浪漫情感。
(B) 你覺得你喜歡一個人，然後一週後就忘了。
(C) 你想要控制一個人，如果他們不聽你的你就生氣。

❸ 以下哪個選項是你在搞不清楚對某人的感覺時應該做的？
(A) 對你所有的感覺採取行動。
(B) 忽略你的感覺，繼續你的人生。
(C) 和你可以信賴的大人討論你的感覺。

選擇題答案：1.B　2.A　3.C

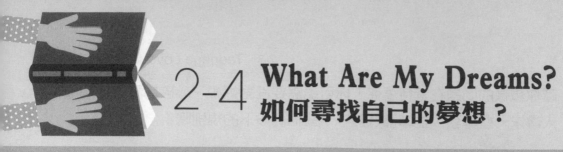

# 2-4 What Are My Dreams?
## 如何尋找自己的夢想？

## Word Bank 夢想

| 字彙 | 音標 | 詞性 | 中譯 |
|------|------|------|------|
| future | ˋfjutʃɚ | n. | 未來 |
| discover | dısˋkʌvɚ | v. | 發現 |
| passion | ˋpæʃən | n. | 熱情 |
| interview | ˋıntɚˌvju | v. | 訪問 |
| speech | spitʃ | n. | 演講 |
| option | ˋɑpʃən | n. | 選擇 |
| horizon | həˋraızn | n. | 地平線 |
| volunteer | ˌvɑlənˋtır | n. | 志工 |
| necessary | ˋnɛsəˌsɛrı | adj. | 必須的 |
| open-minded | ˋopənˋmaındıd | adj. | 開放的 |

Word Bank

## Reading—Teenage Love

 MP3 018

Every day, you show up at school early in the morning. You get overwhelmed by lessons and tests. You leave school at night only to find more books to read and tests to prepare for. You rarely have time to think about the **future** and **discover** your **passion**s. This may be true for most students in Asia.

**Save time for yourself and talk to yourself**

It is very important to find time for yourself, without any distractions from technology. In order to find out what you want to do in the future, you should first know that there is more than one possibility. Keep asking yourself questions. Analyze your hobbies and think about what really makes you happy. Read books and watch **interview**s or **speeches** to find out what people have done and what you can consider doing. There are more job **option**s than you first assume. Travel more if you can, whether in your country or abroad. When you are in a new and unfamiliar environment, you will be provided with many opportunities to think about what you really want. Your **horizons** will be expanded and, with more courage, you will begin to cultivate bigger dreams.

**Meet someone working in the field you are interested in**

If you think you are interested in a certain field, it would be very helpful to speak to someone who is working in that field. You will be able to gain first-hand information on what it is really like and whether it fits the lifestyle you want. For example, if your dream life includes constant travel, it does not make sense to get a job that requires you to stay in the same place every day. Look for opportunities to **volunteer**, visit companies or participate in job shadowing. You can find out if you have romanticized the job. Or you can meet people in the field you are interested in and develop contacts that can maybe help you to apply for jobs or internships in the future.

**Believe in yourself and it is okay to fail.**

Build confidence and believe in yourself. Know that it is always possible for you to get what you want. However, it is also okay to fail. Failures can make you stronger and help you better figure out what you want and what you are good at. Feel comfortable talking about your dreams. If you have difficulty figuring out your dreams, it is not the end of the world. You can imagine the kind of life you want to live and examine what needs to be done for you to live such a life. Take lessons to help you build the **necessary** skills. In fact, you can also choose to stay **open-minded** and just do whatever you feel like trying at the time. You will discover your interests and skills along the journey. At one point, everything you have done will help you achieve your dreams. Remember, "When you want something, the entire universe conspires in helping you to achieve it."

## Multiple Choices 小知識選選看

_____ ❶ Which of the following will NOT help you find your dreams?

(A) Talk to a lot of people and find out what they do.

(B) Stay in the environment I am familiar with.

(C) Volunteer in the field that I am interested in.

_____ ❷ What is probably NOT a reason the author suggests doing job shadowing?

(A) One can see what it is really like to work in the field.

(B) One can meet people in the field.

(C) One can feel more comfortable and stay away from challenges.

_____ ❸ Which of the following is TRUE?

(A) If you want to find your dreams, just keep working and never stop to think.

(B) When you are trying to figure out what you like, avoid failures.

(C) It is important to stay open-minded and try different things to find your passions.

**1** 自然科學和科技

**2** 青少年生活

**3** 世界文化和歷史

**4** 現代發明

每天你很早到學校，被大量的課程與考試給淹沒。晚上你離開學校，發現還有更多的書要讀、考試要準備。你幾乎沒有時間思考未來，發掘自己的熱情，大部分的亞洲學生可能都是過著這樣的生活。

## 保留時間給自己和跟自己對話

一定要留些時間給自己，而且是完全沒有受到科技產品的干擾的時間。如果想找出自己未來想做什麼，首先你應該要知道，選擇不是只有一種。不斷問自己問題，分析你的興趣，想想哪些事情可以讓你真的感到開心。看書、聽訪問或演講，看看別人做過什麼，有沒有自己也想做的。其實可以做的工作比你本來想得還多；如果可以的話，多旅遊，國內或國外旅遊都可以，當你在一個新的、陌生的環境，你就會遇到很多機會可以思考你自己真的想要做的事，你的視野會變得更寬廣，而且有了更多勇氣之後，你會開始培養更大的夢想。

## 認識你有興趣領域的業界人士

如果你覺得你對某個特定領域有興趣，去跟在那個領域工作的人聊一聊會對你很有幫助，你可以得到第一手資訊，知道實際的工作狀況，以及這個工作是否符合你想要的生活型態。如果你夢想中的生活包含不斷地旅遊，那麼找一個需要你每天都留在同一個地方的工作，似乎不太合理。尋找可以做義工、參觀公司或參加「影子工作」的機會，你可以知道你是否把某個工作想得太美好了，或是你可以在你有興趣的領域中認識一些人，建立一些人脈，在未來你要申請工作或實習的時候，可以給你一些幫助。

## 相信自己和「失敗也沒有關係」

建立自信，並相信自己，要知道你是可以得到自己渴望的。但是也要知道，失敗是沒關係的，失敗能讓你變得更堅強，也能幫助你更容易看清自己想要的是什麼，或是擅長的是什麼。你可以輕鬆地談論你的夢想，如果你沒辦法找出你的夢想，那也不是世界末日。你可以想像自己想要過怎樣的生活，分析需要做到哪些事情，才能過這樣的生活，上一些課程，來幫助自己取得必要的技能。其實你也可以選擇保持開放的態度，嘗試任何你當下想要嘗試的事，在這個旅程中，你會發現你的興趣以及專長，在某個時刻，你過去累積的經驗會一起幫助你實現夢想。記得，「當你真心渴望某樣東西，整個宇宙都會聯合起來幫助你。」

## ▶▶ 選擇題中譯

❶ 以下哪個選項無法幫助你找到你的夢想？
(A) 跟很多人聊天，找出他們是做什麼的。
(B) 留在我熟悉的環境。
(C) 在我有興趣的領域裡做義工。

❷ 以下哪個可能不是作者建議進行「影子工作」的原因之一？
(A) 可以看出在一個領域工作真正的情況。
(B) 可以認識在某個領域裡工作的人。
(C) 可以感覺更舒服，可以遠離挑戰。

❸ 以下哪個選項是正確的？
(A) 如果你想要找到夢想，就一直不斷地做，不要停下來想。
(B) 當你在試著找出你喜歡什麼的時候，要避免失敗。
(C) 保持心態的開放是很重要的，嘗試不同的事情來找出你的熱情。

選擇題答案：1.B　2.C　3.C

# 2-5 Cyber-bullying
## 網路霸凌

 **Word Bank 網路霸凌**

| 字彙 | 音標 | 詞性 | 中譯 |
| --- | --- | --- | --- |
| victim | ˈvɪk.tɪm | *n.* | 受害者 |
| Internet | ˈɪn.tə.net | *n.* | 網路 |
| electronic | ɪlɛkˈtrɑnɪk | *adj.* | 電子的 |
| device | dɪˈvaɪs | *v.* | 裝置 |
| privacy | ˈpraɪvəsɪ | *n.* | 隱私 |
| block | blɑk | *v.* | 阻擋 |
| digital | ˈdɪdʒɪt! | *adj.* | 數位的 |
| comfort | ˈkʌmfət | *n.* | 安慰 |
| decision | dɪˈsɪʒən | *n.* | 決定 |
| detect | dɪˈtɛkt | *v.* | 察覺 |

**Word Bank**

# Reading–Cyber-bullying

 MP3 019

You have probably heard of students being bullied at school. Bullying makes the **victim** feel helpless, angry or frustrated. After the appearance of the **Internet**, a new form of bullying surfaced. It is known as cyber-bullying and is even more devastating.

Cyber-bullying can happen any time of the day, as long as there are **electronic device**s and the Internet. Cyber-bullies can use e-mails, social media, or text messages to send unkind words or images. They may even create a website just to threaten or mock their victims. Different from traditional face-to-face bullying, cyber-bullying can quickly become widespread, and the offensive messages can easily "go viral." Victims often become depressed and feel that they cannot escape from the bullies. Sadly, most bullies do these things just for fun.

Cyber-bullying has become more common nowadays. Schools and governments are trying to raise awareness and educate people. Laws and rules have been created to stop cyber-bullying. Scientific studies have shown that young people are more willing to send out hurtful messages than adults. One main reason is that the part of the brain that controls **decision**-making is not fully developed in teenagers.

In fact, this part of the brain will not fully develop before the age of 25.

This has led to an anti-bullying technology that **detect**s offensive messages and reminds people to rethink before they send out such messages. Almost everyone changes their mind after being asked to rethink and chooses not to send out the messages. However, when our brains do not allow us to, let us hope that technology can help us to fight the damage that technology has brought.

To prevent yourself from being cyber-bullied, make sure that your social media account is set to the strongest **privacy** setting so that only your friends and family can see you. If you are unfortunately bullied, try not to fire back. Often times, it only worsens the bullying. You can choose to **block** the bully and make sure you print or take a picture of what the bully has sent you. Report the bully to the website or service provider and to the adults or friends who you can trust.

Cyber-bullies may think they are hiding behind the screen and can never be found. In fact, almost everything one does online leaves **digital** footprints and can be traced. When you witness cyber-bullying, do not join in and become a bully yourself. Do not resend the message. Instead, report the cyber-bullying. You can also provide **comfort** and support to the victims to show them that they are not alone.

## Multiple Choices 小知識選選看

_____ ❶ Which of the following is TRUE about cyber-bullying?

(A) Different from traditional bullying, cyber-bullying can be easily escaped.

(B) Cyber-bullying can happen any time of the day and all year round.

(C) It is impossible to catch cyber-bullies because they do not reveal who they are.

_____ ❷ What can we do when we become victims of cyber-bullying?

(A) Print out what the cyber-bully have sent and report it.

(B) Find the bully and argue with him or her.

(C) Keep what happens to us and do not tell it to anyone.

_____ ❸ Which of the following is NOT mentioned as an attempt to stop cyber-bullying?

(A) Setting up laws and rules to stop cyber-bullying.

(B) Stopping people from using the Internet in public spaces.

(C) Developing technology that stops people from committing cyber-bullying.

## ▶▶ 文章中譯

　　你可能有聽過學生在學校被霸凌，遭到霸凌會讓人感到失去希望、憤怒或挫折。在網路出現之後，一種新型態的霸凌出現了，我們稱之為網路霸凌，而它帶來的毀滅性更加巨大。

　　只要有電子裝置與網路，網路霸凌隨時都可能發生。網路惡霸會使用電子郵件、社交媒體或簡訊來傳送惡意的字眼或圖片，甚至會建立網站，只為了威脅或嘲笑他們的受害者。和傳統面對面的霸凌不同的地方在於，網路霸凌可能會以更快的速度傳播開來，傷人的訊息很可能會「爆紅」。受害者通常變得憂鬱，覺得他們無處可逃，令人遺憾的是大部分的惡霸做這些事純粹只是因為覺得好玩。

　　網路霸凌現在變得越來越常見。學校和政府都努力的在提高意識，教育人們，也有許多法律和規定被創立，以阻止網路霸凌。科學研究顯示年輕人會比成人更喜歡發出傷人的訊息，最主要的原因就是青少年的大腦裡，控管決策的部位還沒完全發育完成；事實上，這個大腦部位直到 25 歲之後才會發育完整。

　　這讓一項防止網路霸凌的科技得以出現，偵測出冒犯人的訊息，並在訊息被寄出之前提醒人們再想一遍，幾乎所有被提醒的人都改變心意，選擇不要寄出訊息。然而，當我們的大腦失控時，希望科技可以幫助減輕同樣由科技帶來的壞處。

　　要避免遭受網路霸凌，首先要確定你在社交網站的隱私設定在最強的保護，只有親朋好友可以看到你。如果不幸遇到網路霸凌，盡量避免回應對方，大部份時候這只會讓霸凌情況變得更嚴重。你可以選擇封鎖霸凌者，並確保你有將霸凌者所寄過的東西印出來或照下來。然後將霸凌事件回報給網站或社交媒體服務提供者，並告訴你可以相信的大人或朋友。

　　網路惡霸可能以為自己躲在螢幕後面，永遠不會有人找到他們。不過其實，一個人在網路做的所有事情幾乎都會留下數位足跡，是可以被找到的。如果你目睹網路霸凌，千萬不要加入，也成為網路惡霸，更不要轉寄那則訊息。你應該檢舉網路霸凌的狀況，你也可以給予受害者鼓勵以及支持，讓他們知道他們並不孤單。

## ▶▶ 選擇題中譯

❶ 以下哪個關於網路霸凌的敘述是正確的？

(A) 不同於傳統的霸凌，網路霸凌更容易脫逃。

(B) 網路霸凌在一整年的任何一天的任何時間都可能發生。

(C) 因為網路霸凌者不透露他們的身份，要抓到他們是不可能的。

❷ 當我們遭受網路霸凌時，可以怎麼做？

(A) 印出網路霸凌者所寄的內容，並通報霸凌。

(B) 找出霸凌者，與他或她爭論。

(C) 將發生的事保密，不告訴任何人。

❸ 以下哪個選項不是文章提及為了阻止網路霸凌所做出的嘗試？

(A) 設立法律與規定來阻止網路霸凌。

(B) 阻止人們在公共場所使用網路。

(C) 發展出可以阻止人們網路霸凌的科技。

選擇題答案：1.B　2.A　3.B

# 2-6 Making New Friends through Online Social Networks 網路交友

## Word Bank 網路交友

| 字彙 | 音標 | 詞性 | 中譯 |
| --- | --- | --- | --- |
| claim | kleɪm | v. | 聲稱 |
| assume | ə`sjum | v. | 假定 |
| account | ə`kaʊnt | n. | 帳號 |
| contradictory | ˌkɑntrə`dɪktərɪ | adj. | 矛盾的 |
| list | lɪst | v. | 列入 |
| scam | `skæm | n. | 騙錢 |
| bother | `bɑðɚ | v. | 打擾 |
| trace | tres | v. | 追蹤 |
| reputation | ˌrɛpjə`teʃən | n. | 名聲 |

**Word Bank**

**Reading-Making New Friends through Online Social Networks**

 MP3 020

Thanks to the rapid improvement of the Internet, teens have found a new way to make friends. They like to use social networks such as Facebook to meet other people. However, not all stories are as wonderful as fairy tales. Since it is so easy to create a false profile in this virtual world, many teens are lured by pedophiles(戀童癖), sex traffickers (非法買賣者) or those with other bad intentions. To prevent tragedies from happening, there are some dos and don'ts of online friendship establishment for teens.

If you want to stay safe when meeting online, please always **assume** the person you are dealing with is not the person he or she **claims** to be unless you really know the person in the real world. Besides, always keep your personal information such as ID numbers private or someone could use it to do something evil. What's more, change your pass word for websites you use very often periodically. Then, you can ensure your **account** safe. Another thing you should do is be real online. It seems somehow **contradictory** to what's mentioned above, but the point here is trying not to cheat anyone. Last but not of least importance is reporting any offensive message to the webmaster to end bullying.

For the things you shouldn't do when making friends

online, not meeting online friends alone is always **listed** in the priority for the reason mentioned at the beginning of the second paragraph. If you really want to do so, please find at least a friend to go with you and meet at a public place like the shopping mall. Besides, do not send money to your online friend or receive money from them.

Then, you can prevent the **scam** from happening. Still, don't accept any friend request send by the one you have no connection at all. By doing so, you can avoid being **bothered** by strange guys. Lastly, don't join the talk about sex or the spread of picture or video with this topic. Since everything can be **traced** on the Internet, your **reputation** will be ruined if found participating in such a thing.

## Multiple Choices 小知識選選看

❶ Which of the following is correct?

(A) Provide your private information to your online friend.

(B) Meet your online friend alone.

(C) Change the password of your most-visited web very often.

❷ Why shouldn't we send money to online friends or receive money from them?

(A) To avoid scam

(B) To avoid being bothered by strangers

(C) To guard our reputation

❸ When finding offensive messages online, you should ____ ____.

(A) report them to webmasters

(B) ignore them

(C) talk to your online friend

　　由於網路快速發展，青少年多了一種交朋友的管道，他們喜歡用像臉書這樣的社群網絡來認識新朋友。然而，不是所有交友都像童話故事般美好。由於偽造身分在虛擬世界中易如反掌，有許多青少年被戀童癖、性販賣者或其它不懷好意的人所引誘。為避免悲劇發生，以下是青少年網路交友應該遵循的規範。

　　如果想在網路交友時確保自身安全，除非你在現實世界中認識這個人，否則請別相信你正在打交道的對象真的是他或她所聲稱的那個身分。此外，請隨時將像身分證字號這類的資訊保密，否則有人會運用這些資訊去做壞事。另外，請定期更換你常使用網站的密碼，這樣的話你就可以確保帳號的安全性。還有一件需要注意的事就是請在網路上提供真實的資訊，這聽起來跟似乎跟之前提到的論點衝突，但這裡的重點在於不要用假資訊去欺騙別人。最後同樣很重要的一點是，如果在網路上發現任何攻擊性言語，請通知網管人員以終止網路霸凌。

　　關於網路交友不該做的事，不單獨和網友見面絕對是列在第一條的優先原則，原因同第二段開頭所述。如果你真的要見網友，請找至少一位朋友陪同，並約在像是購物中心這樣的公共場所見面。此外，不要匯款給網友或是接受網友的金錢餽贈，這樣一來，你就不會被騙錢。再來，不要接受你根本不認識的人的交友請求，這樣做可以防止陌生人來騷擾你。最後，不要加入與性有關的談話或是散佈跟此主題相關的圖片或影片。在網路上做任何事都可以被追查得到，如果參與此類事情，會導致你的名譽受損。

▶▶ **選擇題中譯**

❶ 以下何者正確？

(A) 提供你的私人資訊給網友

(B) 單獨見網友

(C) 經常更換常造訪網站的密碼

................................................................

❷ 為何我們不該匯款給網友或是接受網友的金錢饋贈？

(A) 避免詐騙

(B) 避免被陌生人騷擾

(C) 保護自身名譽

................................................................

❸ 當在網路上發現攻擊性言論，你該_____。

(A) 向網管人員回報

(B) 忽略這些言論

(C) 告訴你的網友

................................................................

選擇題答案：1.C 2.A 3.A

# Part3 世界文化和歷史

　　「讀萬卷書，不如行萬里路。」，學習語言最大的作用就是幫助孩子拓展視野，有機會認識不同的文化。本篇共有十一個單元，橫跨美洲、歐洲和亞洲，帶領孩子認識世界文化、地理和歷史事件，希望這些文章帶給總是待在教室中的孩子一個更寬廣的的世界觀。

# 3-1 Dinosaur Park
## 恐龍公園

 **Word Bank 恐龍**

| 字彙 | 音標 | 詞性 | 中譯 |
|------|------|------|------|
| stroll | strol | *v.* | 散步 |
| extinction | ɪk`stɪŋkʃən | *n.* | 滅絕 |
| global climate change | glob! `klaɪmɪt tʃendʒ | *n.* | 全球氣候變遷 |
| comet | `kɑmɪt | *n.* | 彗星 |
| grand | grænd | *adj.* | 盛大的 |
| abundant | ə`bʌndənt | *adj.* | 豐富的 |
| geological | dʒɪə`ladʒɪk! | *adj.* | 地質的 |
| landscape | `lænd͵skep | *n.* | 景觀 |
| ship | ʃɪp | *v.* | 運送 |
| analysis | ə`næləsɪs | *n.* | 分析 |

**Word Bank**

# Reading–Dinosaur Park

 MP3 021

Are you a dinosaur fan? If so, you should find some time to visit the Dinosaur Park in Canada. When **strolling** in the park, you will feel sorry about the **extinction** of the dinosaurs and start to wonder what had exactly happened 65 million years ago. Was the hit of an asteroid or **comet** or the sudden **global climate change** the final answer? Why did the dinosaurs, once the master of the world, completely disappear from the earth?

The Dinosaur Park, located near Brooks, in the Province of Alberta, Canada, has been popular for years since its **grand** opening is 1955. This park has become more well-known for both being given the honor of United Nations Educational, Scientific and Cultural Organization (UNESCO) World Heritage site in 1979 and one of the most **abundant** dinosaur fossil locations in the world. About 40 dinosaur species have been found here.

The Dinosaur Park is not only a hot tourist spot for dinosaur lovers but also an excellent research site for the dinosaur experts. For dinosaur fans, they can enjoy the exhibits of dinosaur fossils and the **geological** structure inside the Park Center. The unique scenery and the diverse formation of the **landscape are** other must-sees in the park. For dinosaur experts, they can find different kinds of plants and dinosaur fossils there. When discoveries are made, they will be soon **shipped** to museums around the world for further scientific **analysis** and public exhibition.

## Multiple Choices 小知識選選看

❶ When does the Dinosaur Park win the title of World Heritage Site from UNESCO?

(A) 1955

(B) 1979

(C) Not mentioned in the article

❷ How many dinosaur species have been discovered in this park?

(A) About 20

(B) About 30

(C) About 40

❸ When fossils are found in the park, they soon be shipped to museums for _____.

(A) Scientific research

(B) Private collection

(C) Not mentioned in the article.

1 自然科學和科技

2 青少年生活

3 世界文化和歷史

4 現代發明

## ▶▶ 文章中譯

你是恐龍迷嗎？如果是的話，你該找個時間造訪位於加拿大的恐龍公園。當漫步在其中時，你會對恐龍的滅絕感到遺憾，並納悶六千五百萬年前究竟發生了什麼事。小行星或彗星的撞擊或是全球氣候驟變就是最終答案了嗎？為何曾是世界主宰的恐龍會完全從地球上消失呢？

自 1955 年盛大開幕以來，位在加拿大亞伯達省布魯克斯附近的恐龍公園一直廣受歡迎。這座公園在 1979 年獲頒聯合國教科文組織認可之世界遺產，加上這裡號稱是全球最豐富的恐龍化石收藏地點之一，恐龍公園因此更加聲名大噪，有將近 40 種恐龍品種是在此被發現的。

恐龍公園不僅是恐龍迷的熱門旅遊景點，也是恐龍專家絕佳的研究場所。恐龍迷可以欣賞到園區中心內恐龍化石與地質結構的展覽品；可別錯過戶外獨特的風景與多樣化的地質景觀。恐龍專家則可以在公園內找到不同植物與恐龍的化石，一旦他們有所收穫，這些化石很快就會被送往世界各地的博物館做進一步的科學分析與公開展示。

▶▶ **選擇題中譯**

❶ 恐龍公園於何時獲頒聯合國教科文組織世界遺產的殊榮?

(A) 1955 年

(B) 1979 年

(C) 文章中未提到

❷ 恐龍公園中至今已發現多少種恐龍?

(A) 約 20 種

(B) 約 30 種

(C) 約 40 種

❸ 當在園區發現化石後,這些化石會快速送往博物館_____。

(A) 做科學研究

(B) 當私人收藏

(C) 文章中未提及

選擇題答案:1.B　2.C　3.A

# 3-2 The Dead Sea
## 死海

 **Word Bank 死海**

| 字彙 | 音標 | 詞性 | 中譯 |
|---|---|---|---|
| concentration | ˌkɑnsɛnˋtreʃən | n. | 濃度 |
| salinity | səˋlɪnətɪ | n. | 鹽度 |
| float | flot | v. | 漂浮 |
| resort | rɪˋzɔrt | n. | 渡假勝地 |
| breathtaking | ˋbrɛθˌtekɪŋ | adj. | 令人屏息的 |
| composition | ˌkɑmpəˋzɪʃən | n. | 成分 |
| sink | sɪŋk | v. | 下沉 |
| cosmetic | kɑzˋmɛtɪk | adj. | 化妝用的 |
| characteristics | ˌkærəktəˋrɪstɪk | n. | 特性 |
| attraction | əˋtrækʃən | n. | 吸引力 |

**Word Bank**

# Reading—The Dead Sea

 MP3 022

Have you ever heard a place in the Middle East named The Dead Sea? If so, do you know why people call it "Dead" Sea? And is it really a sea? Does it cause any harm or death if we jump into the water there?

In fact, The Dead Sea is a salt water lake located between Jordan and Israel. Its name comes from Hebrew, meaning "sea of salt". Being about 400 meters deep, the Dead Sea is the deepest landlocked lake with the highest **concentration** of salt in the world. The high **salinity** prevents life forms like fish from surviving here, so this lake is commonly called "Dead" Sea.

Though the Dead Sea isn't a proper place for creatures to live, people won't get hurt if they stay in the water. When jumping into the Dead Sea, you don't have to worry about **sink**ing down because the high salinity enables you to **float** on the surface.

Nowadays, The Dead Sea has become a well-known health **resort**. Tourists can visit some purely historic spots nearby, enjoy the **breathtaking** natural scenery, and float on the "seawater" in the bathing areas. In addition, many visitors come here for its unique products of both healing and beauty properties. The **composition** of the salts and minerals in the water can be used to cure chronic diseases, such as arthritis and the deposits of the black mud from the sea can be materials for **cosmetic** products. With so many amazing **characteristics**, no wonder it has become such a popular tourist **attraction**.

## Multiple Choices 小知識選選看

❶ Which of the following is not correct?

(A) The Dead Sea is a sea between Jordan and Israel.

(B) The Dead Sea is about 400m in depth.

(C) The Dead Sea is a dangerous place which people should not come near.

❷ Why creatures can't live in The Dead Sea?

(A) Because the salinity of the water is high.

(B) Because the water is extremely dirty.

(C) Because the water is extremely hot.

❸ The material in the Dead Sea can be used in_____.

(A) Product with healing properties

(B) Cosmetics products

(C) All of above

　　你有聽過中東有個地方叫做死海嗎？如果有的話，你知道為什麼那裡被稱為「死」海嗎？死海真的是海嗎？如果我們跳進死海裡會受傷或是死亡嗎？

　　事實上，死海是位在約旦和以色列之間的鹹水湖。其名稱源自希伯來文，意思是「鹽之海」。死海水深約 400 公尺，是世界上最深且鹽度最高的內陸湖。高鹽度使得像是魚這類的生物無法在湖裡生存，因此這座湖被稱做「死」海。雖然死海不是個適合生物居住的好地方，但人也不會因為泡在死海水裡就受傷。當你跳進死海中，不用擔心會下沉，因為高鹽度的湖水會讓你漂浮在水面上。

　　今日死海已經成為著名的療養勝地。遊客可以參觀附近正統的歷史古蹟、欣賞令人屏息的天然美景，還可以漂浮在泡水區的「海水」上。此外，也有許多遊客是為了兼具治療與美容功能的獨特產品而來到死海的。湖水中的鹽與礦物質可以治療像是關節炎這類的慢性疾病，湖中沉積的黑泥則可做為化妝品的原料。有這些驚人的特性，難怪死海會成為如此熱門的觀光景點。

## ▶▶ 選擇題中譯

❶ 以下何者不正確?

(A) 死海位在約旦與以色列之間

(B) 死海深度約 400 公尺

(C) 死海是個人類不應靠近的危險之地

- - - - - - - - - - - - - - - - - - - - - - - - - - - - - - -

❷ 為何生物無法在死海中生存?

(A) 因為水的鹽度高

(B) 因為水很髒

(C) 因為水很燙

- - - - - - - - - - - - - - - - - - - - - - - - - - - - - - -

❸ 死海中的物質可用來_____.

(A) 製作具療效的產品

(B) 製作化妝品

(C) 以上皆是

- - - - - - - - - - - - - - - - - - - - - - - - - - - - - - -

選擇題答案：1.C　2.A　3.C

1 自然科學和科技

2 青少年生活

3 世界文化和歷史

4 現代發明

# 3-3 Easter Island
## 復活節島

 **Word Bank 復活節島**

| 字彙 | 音標 | 詞性 | 中譯 |
|------|------|------|------|
| **explorer** | ɪk`splorə | n. | 探險家 |
| **volcanic** | vɑl`kænɪk | adj. | 火山的 |
| **inland** | `ɪnlənd | n. | 內陸 |
| **civilization** | ˌsɪvḷə`zeʃən | n. | 文明 |
| **ancestor** | `ænsɛstə | n. | 祖先 |
| **status** | `stetəs | n. | 身分地位 |
| **fatal** | `fetḷ | adj. | 致命的 |
| **tragedy** | `trædʒədɪ | n. | 悲劇 |
| **puzzle** | `pʌzḷ | v. | 迷惑 |
| **majestic** | mə`dʒɛstɪk | adj. | 雄偉的 |

**Word Bank**

# Reading—Easter Island

MP3 023

1 自然科學和科技

2 青少年生活

3 世界文化和歷史

4 現代發明

Have you ever heard of an island called Easter Island? Do you know the origin of its name? Do you know why this island has become so famous?

Easter Island is a tiny Chilean island in the southeastern Pacific Ocean at the southeastern-most point of Polynesia. Polynesia, the name of the island group, was made by European **explorers** in the 18th century. Because they found this island on Easter, they named it "Easter Island." In addition, according to languages spoken on this island, it is also called "Rapa Nui Island".

The main reason why this island has become well-known is the discovery of giant god-like statues made of **volcanic** rocks named Moai. Each huge statue wears a crown, has very long ears, and weighs up to 14 tons, facing **inland**, away from the sea. The Heads were probably built sometime between 1,000 and 1,100 AD though the Island's earliest **civilization** might have started as early as 400 AD.

They were believed to have represented the tribe's **ancestors**, and probably the **status** symbols of the powerful chiefs. However, the legend had it that sometime during the late seventeenth century, the tribe that built the statues was completely destroyed in a **fatal** battle, and the **tragedy** brought a ghostly air to the Island and its inhabitants.

Till today, the exact purpose of building the huge sculptures and how they were mounted in place still **puzzle** the world a lot. Before the puzzles are finally solved, the **majestic** Easter Island Moai will leave us endless room for imagination.

## Multiple Choices 小知識選選看

❶ Why European explorers name this island Easter?
(A) Because the island is located in the east
(B) Because they arrive at/on this island on Easter
(C) Because the inhabitant here speak Easter Language

❷ Which of the following description is wrong?
(A) Moai is made of wood and mud.
(B) Moai is probably built sometime between 1,000 and 1,100 AD.
(C) Moai wear a crown.

❸ When does Easter Island become famous?
(A) The 4th century
(B) The 11th century
(C) The 18th century

　　你有聽過一個名為復活節島的小島嗎？你知道這個島為什麼叫復活節島嗎？你知道這個島為什麼這麼有名嗎？

　　復活節島是智利的一座小島，位在東南太平洋的玻里尼西亞極東南點上。玻里尼西亞這個群島的名字是由 18 世紀的歐洲探險家所命名，由於是在復活節時抵達，便以此節日做為島名。此外，若依照島上所使用的語言，也可稱其為「拉帕努伊島」。

　　此島變得遠近馳名主要是因為在此發現了許多用火山岩製成，名為摩艾的巨大神像。每尊雕像都帶著皇冠、擁有長耳、重達 14 噸以上且全都面陸背海。儘管島上最早的文明可能起源於西元 400 年，但這些頭像可能是在西元 1000 年到 1100 年間才被建造出來。人們相信它們代表著部落的祖先，可能是極具權勢酋長的地位象徵。然而，有傳聞指出 17 世紀末期的某個時刻，建造這些雕像的部落在一次致命的戰役當中全數被殲滅了，而這個悲劇將復活島和當地居民籠罩於一股鬼魅般的氣氛中。

　　時至今日，人們仍無法了解建造巨型雕像的確切目的，以及它們是如何被搬移至定位的。在謎底最終揭曉前，宏偉的復活島摩艾雕像將永遠留給世人無限想像空間。

## ▶▶ 選擇題中譯

❶ 為何歐洲探險者將此島命名為復活節島？

(A) 因為這個島位在東方

(B) 因為他們在復活節時抵達該島

(C) 因為居民說復活節語

- - - - - - - - - - - - - - - - - - - - - - - - - - - - - - - - - - - - - - - -

❷ 以下哪個描述是錯誤的？

(A) 摩艾雕像是由木頭與泥所製成

(B) 摩艾雕像可能在西元前 1100 年到 1000 年前被建造

(C) 摩艾雕像頭戴皇冠

- - - - - - - - - - - - - - - - - - - - - - - - - - - - - - - - - - - - - - - -

❸ 復活節島從何時開始變得有名？

(A) 4 世紀

(B) 11 世紀

(C) 18 世紀

- - - - - - - - - - - - - - - - - - - - - - - - - - - - - - - - - - - - - - - -

選擇題答案：1.B　2.A　3.C

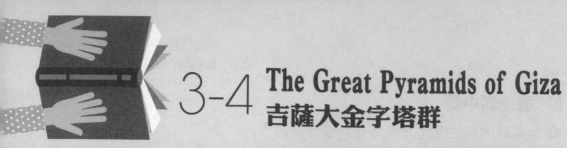

# 3-4 The Great Pyramids of Giza
# 吉薩大金字塔群

 **Word Bank** 吉薩大金字塔群

| 字彙 | 音標 | 詞性 | 中譯 |
|---|---|---|---|
| spectacles | `spɛktək!z | n. | 奇觀 |
| Sphinx | sfɪŋks | | 獅身人面像 |
| Egyptian | ɪˋdʒɪpʃən | adj. | 埃及的 |
| pyramid | ˋpɪrəmɪd | n. | 金字塔 |
| corridor | ˋkɔrɪdə | n. | 通道 |
| chamber | ˋtʃembə | n. | 房間 |
| coffin | ˋkɔfɪn | n. | 棺材 |
| alien | ˋelɪən | n. | 外星人 |
| mathematical | ˌmæθəˋmætɪk! | adj. | 數學的 |
| measurement | ˋmɛʒəmənt | n. | 測量 |

**Word Bank**

# Reading-The Great Pyramids of Giza

 MP3 024

Do you know what Seven Wonders of the Ancient World is? If so, you must know the Great **Pyramids** of Giza in Cairo, Egypt. Of the original Seven Wonders, the Great Pyramids of Giza is the oldest one as well as only one remains today. Therefore, it is not only an important historic heritage of **Egyptian** but also the most impressive **spectacles** of human civilization.

## The structure of The Great Pyramids of Giza

The Great Pyramids of Giza mainly refers the three big pyramids which guarded by the statue of the **Sphinx**. They were built as royal tombs for Pharaohs between 2,575 BC and 2,465 BC. However, they probably also served ritualistic (儀式的) purposes and astronomical (天文學的) functions. The largest of them held the record for the world's tallest pyramid for its height of 481 feet.

It is estimated that it took at least 20 years to complete the construction of pyramids, and it required the labor of a hundred thousand workers moving 2.6 million blocks of stone into the site. The inner part of the pyramid is as astonishing (驚人的) as its appearance. Inside the pyramids, there were elaborate **corridors** and huge **chambers**, with jewelry, stone blocks, and cutting tools found. More surprisingly, the **coffin** chamber for pharaoh is perfectly located at the center of the pyramid.

Till today, amazing things about the Great Pyramids of Giza still puzzle the world a lot. No wonder people used to think that only the highly intelligent **aliens** from the outer space could have possibly created the huge and perfect pyramids. Otherwise, it would be impossible for the ancient Egyptians, supposedly with limited **mathematical** and astronomical (天文學的) knowledge, to have achieved the difficult task of making the exact **measurements**.

## Multiple Choices 小知識選選看

❶ Which of the following is correct?

(A) The Great Pyramids of Giza is built as the royal tomb for Pharaoh.

(B) The Great Pyramids of Giza is the biggest pyramid in the world.

(C) The Great Pyramids of Giza is in Alexandra, Egypt.

❷ The Great Pyramids of Giza is guarded by_____.

(A) The statue of alien from the outer space

(B) The statue of Pharaoh

(C) The statue of Sphinx

❸ How long does it take to The Great Pyramids of Giza according to the estimation?

(A)10 years

(B)20 years

(C)30 years

1 自然科學和科技

2 青少年生活

3 世界文化和歷史

4 現代發明

你熟悉古代世界的七大奇蹟嗎?如果是的話,你肯定知道位在埃及開羅的吉薩大金字塔群。在最初的世界七大奇蹟中,吉薩大金字塔群是最古老也是目前唯一現存的。因此它不僅是埃及重要的歷史遺產,也是人類文明最令人印象深刻的奇觀。

吉薩大金塔群主要指的是由人面獅身像所看守的三座大金字塔,這些金字塔於西元前 2575 年到 2465 年間被建造為法老的皇家陵墓,但金字塔同時也可能具有儀式或天文方面的功能。金字塔群中最大的那座以標高 481 英呎榮登全球最高金字塔。據估計,完成這項建築至少得花費 20 年,同時需要動用十萬名工人合力搬動 260 萬塊的石塊到達建築地點。

金字塔內部與其外觀一樣令人瞠目結舌。塔內有設計精密的複雜通道以及巨大的房間,此外還發現了珠寶、石塊以及切割工具。更令人驚訝的是,法老的墓穴竟然完美地位在金字塔的正中心。

時至今日,吉薩大金字塔群仍有許多世人無法理解的驚人之處。難怪過去有人認為只有來自外太空具有高度智慧的外星人才有可能創造出如此巨大而且完美的金字塔。否則,對於數學和天文知識有限的古埃及人來說,理應無法完成如此精準的測量。

▶▶ **選擇題中譯**

❶ 以下何者正確?

(A) 吉薩大金字塔群是法老王的皇家陵墓

(B) 吉薩大金字塔群是世上最大的金字塔

(C) 吉薩大金字塔群位於埃及的亞歷山大

. . . . . . . . . . . . . . . . . . . . . . . . . . . . . . . . . . . . . . . . . .

❶ 吉薩大金字塔群是由誰所看守?

(A) 外星人的雕像

(B) 法老的雕像

(C) 人面獅身像

. . . . . . . . . . . . . . . . . . . . . . . . . . . . . . . . . . . . . . . . . .

❷ 根據估計,完成吉薩大金字塔群需要幾年?

(A) 10 年

(B) 20 年

(C) 30 年

. . . . . . . . . . . . . . . . . . . . . . . . . . . . . . . . . . . . . . . . . .

選擇題答案:1.A 2.A 3.B

# 3-5 Chinese Immigration 華人移民潮

## Word Bank 華人移民潮

| 字彙 | 音標 | 詞性 | 中譯 |
|---|---|---|---|
| decade | ˋdɛked | n. | 十年 |
| mining | ˋmaɪnɪŋ | n. | 採礦 |
| refugee | ˌrɛfjʊˋdʒi | n. | 難民 |
| hostile | ˋhɑstɪl | adj. | 有敵意的 |
| alliance | əˋlaɪəns | n. | 同盟 |
| professional | prəˋfɛʃən | n. | 專業人士 |
| bland | blænd | adj. | 溫和的 |
| exotic | ɛgˋzɑtɪk | adj. | 異國情調的 |
| ingredient | ɪnˋgridɪənt | n. | 原料 |
| cuisine | kwɪˋzin | n. | 佳餚 |

Word Bank

# Reading—Chinese Immigration

 MP3 025

When traveling in the United States, you may find there are so many Chinatowns in cities. Chinatowns represent not only the strength of Chinese immigrants but also the adjustment of Chinese dishes.

**The three waves of Chinese immigration in the USA.**

There were three waves of Chinese immigration to the USA in American history. The first wave happened in the early 19th century. At that time, Chinese immigrants usually worked as cheap labor for transcontinental (橫貫大陸的) railroads and the **mining** industry. During the economic crisis in the 1870s, white Americans blamed the Chinese for taking their jobs. Anti-Chinese movements forced Chinese people to become **refugees**, leaving them no choice but to escape to Chinatowns.

The **hostile** opposition even made Congress passed the Chinese Exclusion Act in 1882. Following this, Chinese immigration was prohibited for a **decade.** The second wave began with the **alliance** between the United States and China during WWII in 1943. In this phase, most immigrants worked in restaurants or laundries. The third wave began in the 1980s when Chinese migrated to the US as students and

**professionals**.

## How Chinese food changed in the USA

For the early Chinese immigrants, especially those who arrived in the second wave, opening a small restaurant was one of the most common ways to make a living. To get into the market, it was necessary to adjust the taste of the food. It should be **exotic** yet acceptable for Americans. To achieve this goal, the sauce was **blander,** thicker, and sweeter. Besides, western style **ingredients** such as broccoli and onions replaced leafy vegetables. Take General Tso's Chicken (左宗棠雞) as an example. It should be a spicy and salty chicken dish. However, it tastes sweet and sour when you find this **cuisine** in the USA now.

# Multiple Choices 小知識選選看

❶ In the second wave of immigration, Chinese people usually work in _____ in the USA.
(A) restaurants and laundry
(B) railway construction site
(C) schools

❷ To get into the American market, the Chinese food in the USA will taste _____.
(A) spicier
(B) sweeter
(C) saltier

❸ How many waves of Chinese immigration to the USA in American history?
(A) one
(B) two
(C) three

自然科學和科技 **1**

青少年生活 **2**

世界文化和歷史 **3**

現代發明 **4**

## ▶▶ 文章中譯

如果你曾到過美國旅行，就會發現各大城市都有中國城。中國城不僅代表了華裔移民的堅忍，也表現出有別於傳統中華料理的特色。

### 美國的三次華人移民潮

美國歷史上共有三次華人移民潮。第一次始於 19 世紀早期，那時華裔移民大多在橫貫大陸鐵路工程及礦業當廉價勞工。1870 年經濟危機時，美國白人怪罪華裔勞工搶了他們飯碗。排華運動使得華人淪落為難民，只能逃往中國城。強烈的反對聲浪甚至迫使國會於 1882 年通過排華條款，自此禁止華人移民長達十年。第二波移民潮始於 1943 年中美於二次大戰時結盟，此時期多數移民在餐廳或是洗衣店工作。第三波移民潮則始於 1980 年代，這時華人多赴美求學或是擔任專業人士。

### 中華料理在美國的演變

對早期的華裔移民而言，特別是趕上第二波移民潮的那些人，開間小餐廳是最常見用來維持生計的方式。為了要打進美國市場，他們在餐點風味上做了許多調整。口味上必須保留異國風情但又能為美國人所接受。為了達到這個目標，醬料味道變得更溫和，但濃稠度提高且比原先更甜。此外，更加入了西式食材，例如花椰菜及洋蔥來取代葉菜類蔬菜。以左宗棠雞為例，這是道以鹹與辣著稱的雞肉料理，但當你在美國品嚐這道菜時，它的口味卻是甜中帶酸的。

▶▶ **選擇題中譯**

❶ 在第二波移民潮時，在美國的華裔大多在_____工作。

(A) 餐廳或洗衣店

(B) 鐵道工程工地

(C) 學校

❷ 為了打進當地市場，在美國的中華料理嚐起來會_____。

(A) 更辣

(B) 更甜

(C) 更鹹

❸ 在美國歷史上總共有幾波華人移民潮?

(A) 一波

(B) 兩波

(C) 三波

選擇題答案: 1.A　2.B　3.C

1 自然科學和科技

2 青少年生活

3 世界文化和歷史

4 現代發明

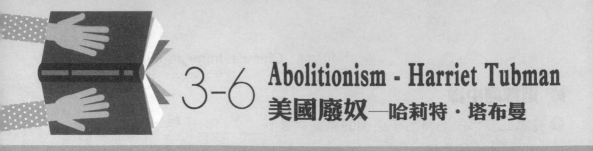

# 3-6 Abolitionism - Harriet Tubman
# 美國廢奴—哈莉特·塔布曼

 **Word Bank 黑奴**

| 字彙 | 音標 | 詞性 | 中譯 |
|---|---|---|---|
| determination | dɪˌtɝməˋneʃən | n. | 決心 |
| sibling | ˋsɪblɪŋ | n. | 同胞 |
| bounty | ˋbaʊntɪ | n. | 獎金 |
| fugitive | ˋfjudʒətɪv | n. | 逃亡者 |
| capture | ˋkæptʃɚ | v. | 逮捕 |
| warehouse | ˋwɛrˌhaʊs | n. | 倉庫 |
| rebel | ˋrɛb! | n. | 反叛者（此處特指美國南北戰爭中南方士兵） |
| biography | baɪˋɑgrəfɪ | n. | 傳記 |
| expedition | ˌɛkspɪˋdɪʃən | n. | 遠征 |
| liberation | ˌlɪbəˋreʃən | n. | 解放 |

**Word Bank**

## Reading—Abolitionism-Harriet Tubman

 MP3 026

Though born as a slave, Harriet Tubman firmly believed that all African Americans should be free. She once remarked "Every great dream begins with a dreamer. Always remember, you have within you the strength, the patience and the passion to reach for the stars to change the world." These words clearly showed her **determination** to rescue as many **siblings** as she can.

### Joining the secret organization – Underground Railroad

After Tubman escaped from the field alone in 1849, she started to think about how to aid her family and friends to regain freedom. Joining the secret organization named Underground Railroad was her solution. With their help, Tubman returned to the South no fewer than 19 times even many **bounty** hunters was chasing her and helped hundreds of other blacks to escape to Canada. And what more important is none of the **fugitives** he guided was ever **captured**.

When the Civil War broke out, Tubman assisted the Union Army as a nurse, a scout (偵查兵), and a spy. She was also the leader of a troop made of local blacks to venture into **rebel** territory to gather information such as the location of **warehouses** and ammunition depots. With this crucial information, Colonel James Montgomery made several **expeditions** to southern areas to destroy supplies.

### Be regarded as the "Moses of her people"

After the war, Tubman returned to New York to live with her family and to help escaped black to begin their new life. She earned money by making speeches and selling her **biography**. Then, she finally had her own house and built a nursing home for the elderly blacks. Tubman devotes almost her entire life to the **liberation** of the black slave, so she truly deserves being nicknamed as "Moses of her people."

# Multiple Choices 小知識選選看

❶ Who or which organization help Tubman to the South to rescue her siblings?
(A) Underground Railroad
(B) Colonel James Montgomery
(C) Not mentioned in the article

❷ The troop Tubman lead is responsible for _____.
(A) gathering the information in the rebel territory
(B) maintain the supplies
(C) making crucial decisions

❸ Tubman is nicknamed "Moses of her people" mainly for her great contribution to _____.
(A) Union army
(B) black slave liberation
(C) the secret organization Underground Railroad

## ▶▶ 文章中譯

儘管生為奴隸，哈莉特•塔布曼深信所有非裔美國人都該是自由的。她曾說過「每一個偉大的夢想都由一個夢想者開始。永遠記住，你內在擁有力量、耐心及熱忱可以完成壯舉改變世界」，這段話清楚地表現她竭盡所能解救同胞的決心。

### 加入秘密組織 – 地下鐵道

在塔布曼於 1849 年獨自逃離牧場後，她開始思考如何讓她的家人朋友重獲自由。她想到了一個解決辦法：加入名為地下鐵道的秘密組織。有了組織的協助，儘管塔布曼被一票賞金獵人緊咬不放，她還是成功潛回南方不下 19 次，成功幫助數以百計的黑人逃往加拿大。更重要的是，在她的帶領下，沒有任何逃亡者被捕。

當南北戰爭爆發時，塔曼在聯邦軍中身兼護士、偵察兵與間諜三種身分。她同時還領導一支由當地黑人所組成的軍隊，這支軍隊負責潛入叛軍領地蒐集有關倉庫與彈藥庫地點的情報。這些關鍵情報帶來莫大的助益，使詹姆士蒙哥馬利上校屢次深入南方成功切斷敵軍補給線。

### 被視為「黑人的摩西」

戰後塔曼回到紐約與家人同住，並幫助重獲自由的黑人展開新生活。塔曼靠四處演講及販賣自傳來賺錢。後來，她終於買下屬於自己的房子，並為黑人長者建了一座安養院。終其一生，塔布曼幾乎將她所有時間都奉獻給黑奴的解放，因此她的綽號「黑人的摩西」可以說是實至名歸。

▶▶ **選擇題中譯**

❶ 誰或是哪個組織幫助塔布曼回到南方營救她的同胞**?**

(A) 地下鐵道

(B) 蒙哥馬利上校

(C) 文章中未提及

. . . . . . . . . . . . . . . . . . . . . . . . . . . . . . . . . . . . . . . . . . . . . . . . . . . . . . . . . . . .

❷ 塔布曼所領導的軍隊是負責_____。

(A) 蒐集叛軍領地的情資

(B) 維持補給

(C) 做重大決定

. . . . . . . . . . . . . . . . . . . . . . . . . . . . . . . . . . . . . . . . . . . . . . . . . . . . . . . . . . . .

❸ 塔布曼被稱為黑人的摩西，主要是因為她在_____的卓越貢獻。

(A) 聯邦軍

(B) 黑奴解放

(C) 秘密組織地下鐵道

. . . . . . . . . . . . . . . . . . . . . . . . . . . . . . . . . . . . . . . . . . . . . . . . . . . . . . . . . . . .

選擇題答案：1.A　2.A　3.B

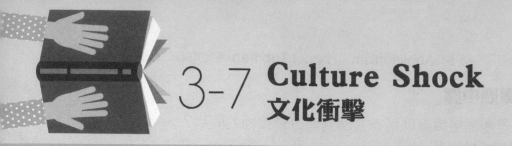

# 3-7 Culture Shock
## 文化衝擊

## Word Bank 文化衝擊

| 字彙 | 音標 | 詞性 | 中譯 |
| --- | --- | --- | --- |
| country | `kʌntrɪ | n. | 國家 |
| environment | ɪn`vaɪrənmənt | n. | 環境 |
| adventure | əd`vɛntʃɚ | n. | 冒險 |
| pressure | `prɛʃɚ | n. | 壓力 |
| homesick | `hom͵sɪk | adj. | 思鄉的 |
| overcome | ͵ovɚ`kʌm | v. | 克服 |
| familiar | fə`mɪljɚ | adj. | 熟悉的 |
| embrace | ɪm`bres | v. | 擁抱 |
| deal with | dil wɪð | ph. | 處理 |
| mind | maɪnd | n. | 心 |

Word Bank

# Reading–Culture Shock

 MP3 027

A traveler from the U.S. arrives in Taiwan. Hungry as he is, he walks into a restaurant to get something to eat. When he sits down, he is extremely shocked to see a man putting a chicken foot in his mouth, chewing, and looking content. He cannot believe what he is seeing. The American traveler is experiencing what is known as "culture shock." Culture shock is the feeling of confusion one feels when traveling or moving to another **country** or social **environment**. There are typically four stages of culture shock.

## The 1st to 4th stages of culture shock

The first stage is the "honeymoon" stage. When a person arrives in the new environment, he or she is very positive. Everything, from the food to the people, excites the person and he cannot wait to begin the **adventure**. The person might learn the language, visit new places, meet different people and try local food. This phase may last for a couple of months until the person is faced with more problems and goes into the second stage. What follows the honeymoon stage is the "frustration" stage. It is also called the "negotiation" stage and is probably the most difficult stage.

During this phase, the person may start to feel the difficulty in communicating using the local language. Perhaps he or she cannot get used to certain kinds of food and may have trouble understanding all the cultural rules. All the **pressure** combined with **homesick** feelings can be very hard to deal with. One may suddenly become very sick, lose sleep, and feel angry about everything. The second stage may last months.

After struggling through the second stage, one may choose to leave the new environment or stay to enter the third stage. The third stage of culture shock is "adjustment." This is a stage where the person has **overcome** the problems and feels more **familiar** with whatever he or she used to find challenging. He or she may start to have a better command of the language and start making more friends. The person feels more at home and is welcomed by the 4th stage, the "acceptance" stage. Arriving at this stage may take one or many years. One may not completely understand the culture, but feels very comfortable in the new environment. He stops comparing the new culture with the old one. The person **embrace**s both cultures and develops a new identity for him or herself.

## The importance of learning to deal culture shock

We are all bound to experience culture shock at some point in life. It is important that we learn how to **deal with** it. First of all, you can learn the new language. Learning how to speak the local language will help you get through culture shock a lot faster. Secondly, meet new friends. One can get used to a new culture more quickly when having some local friends around. Finally, keep an open **mind**. Know that you may never understand the new culture the way you understand your own, and it is okay. Ask people when you feel confused. Try to stay positive and be open to new challenges.

## Multiple Choices 小知識選選看

_____ ❶ Which of the following scenario fits the frustration stage?

(A) One cannot understand what people say in class.

(B) One is excited to explore the new country.

(C) One feels very familiar with the new culture.

_____ ❷ How do people usually feel when they enter the third stage?

(A) very angry

(B) more comfortable

(C) very sad

_____ ❸ How can people overcome culture shock?

(A) Keep comparing a new culture with their cultures

(B) Go to a language school and learn the local language

(C) Only stay with people from their countries

1 自然科學和科技

2 青少年生活

3 世界文化和歷史

4 現代發明

173

## ▶▶ 文章中譯

　　有個美國來的遊客抵達了台灣，肚子很餓，他走進了餐廳，想找點什麼來吃。當他坐下的時候，他被嚇到了，旁邊的男人竟然把雞爪放進嘴裡咀嚼，看起來很滿足，他沒辦法相信眼前所見的一切。這位美國的遊客感受到的就是所謂的「文化衝擊」。文化衝擊指的是，人因為旅行或遷移到另一個國家或社交環境時，出現的困惑感，文化衝擊通常可以分為四個階段。

### 文化衝擊：第一階段到第四階段

　　第一個階段是「蜜月期」。當一個人初到新的環境時，保有非常正面的態度，從食物到人等所有的事物都讓他感到興奮，他等不及要展開新的冒險。他會去學當地的語言、參觀沒去過的地方、認識不同的人，並品嚐當地的食物。這個階段可能會持續好幾個月，直到他遇到更多的問題，而進入了第二個階段。在蜜月期之後，會出現「挫折期」，或稱「抗拒期」，這可能是最困難的時期。在這個階段，一個人可能會開始感覺到使用當地語言溝通的困難，這個人也可能無法適應某些食物，或無法了解全部的文化禮儀。所有的壓力再加上想家，可能會很難面對。人可能會突然極度心煩意亂、失眠、對所有事物感到憤怒。這第二個階段可能會持續好幾個月。

　　在掙扎經過第二個階段之後，人可能會選擇離開這個新環境，或是留下來，進入第三階段。第三個階段是「調整期」，在這個階段時，一個人已經克服了困難，對於先前感到很有挑戰性的事物，已經開始覺得熟悉了，可能當地語言已經說得比較好了，並且開始結交更多朋友。現在這個人已經比較自在了，並迎向第四階段「融入期」。要來到這個階段可能要花一年，甚至好幾年。一個人或許還沒完全了解當地文化，但在這個新環境已經非常的自在，他不再將新文化和舊文化做比較，而是擁抱兩個文化，並為自己發展出新的身份。

## 學會面對文化衝擊的重要性

　　我們在人生的某個階段必定會經歷文化衝擊，學會如何面對文化衝擊是很重要的。首先，你可以學習當地的新語言，學會說當地的語言會幫助你更快走出文化衝突。其次，去認識新朋友，當周遭有當地朋友時，一個人能更快習慣新文化。最後，保持開放的心態，要知道你可能永遠都不會像了解自己原本的文化一般，了解新的文化，但也沒關係，感到困惑的時候，就去問人，試著保持樂觀，並勇於接受新的挑戰。

## ▶▶ 選擇題中譯

❶ 以下哪個情形最符合「挫折期」？
(A) 一個人無法了解人們在課堂上講什麼。
(B) 一個人對於可以探索新國家感到興奮。
(C) 一個人對於新文化感到很熟悉。

❷ 人們在進入第三階段時，通常會有什麼感覺？
(A) 很生氣
(B) 比較舒適
(C) 非常傷心

❸ 人們怎麼做，可以克服文化衝擊？
(A) 一直把新文化和自己的文化做比較。
(B) 去語言學校學習當地語言。
(C) 只和自己國家的人相處。

選擇題答案：1.A　2.B　3.B

# 3-8 Dabbawala
## 印度終極快遞系統

 **Word Bank 印度終極快遞**

| 字彙 | 音標 | 詞性 | 中譯 |
|---|---|---|---|
| lunchbox | ˋlʌntʃbɑks | n. | 午餐盒 |
| system | ˋsɪstəm | n. | 系統 |
| container | kənˋtenɚ | n. | 容器 |
| deliver | dɪˋlɪvɚ | v. | 遞送 |
| collect | kəˋlɛkt | v. | 收集 |
| station | ˋsteʃən | n. | 車站 |
| manage to | ˋmænɪdʒ tu | ph. | 設法… |
| destination | dɛstəˋneʃən | n. | 目的地 |
| technology | tɛkˋnɑlədʒɪ | n. | 科技 |
| error | ˋɛrɚ | n. | 錯誤 |

**Word Bank**

# Reading–Dabbawala

 MP3 028

Imagine this: on a very busy street, you see a man in a white hat carrying 30 four-layer **lunchbox**es on his bicycle. He rushes through the city traffic to a train station to pass on the lunchboxes. He is an important part of the most complex and efficient delivery **system** in India, mainly in Mumbai.

The man is called a dabbawala because he carries dabbas, food **container**s used in India, usually of three or four layers and made of aluminum. The dabbawalas form an amazing system just to **deliver** lunches to offices or schools. Back in the 1890s, there were very few restaurants in Mumbai and the many different ethnic groups and castes in India each had their own dietary needs. With a growing number of office workers commuting a long distance, going home for the preferred home-cooked meals was impossible. Wanting to have hot home-made lunch from his wife, a man started the delivery service, which later turns into an association. The dabbawalas in the association (社團) do not have bosses and help each other complete delivery tasks.

**A dabba changes hands at least three times before arriving at the destinations.**

The most amazing part of the dabbawala system is that a dabba changes hands at least three times. Early in the morning, people prepare lunch for their loved ones and put it in dabbas. At around 9 o'clock, dabbawalas start **collect**ing lunchboxes from each home in the area they are responsible for. They go up and down, from buildings to buildings. They put all the lunchboxes on their bicycles. The bicycles are specially made to be heavier than regular bicycles so they can carry a lot of lunchboxes. One dabbawala can be carrying up to 40 containers at one time.

Almost two hours later, dabbawalas are on their way to the nearest train **station** and give the lunchboxes to the next dabbawalas going to different parts of the city. They have to carry up to up to 60 dabbas in their head crates and **manage to** find the right trains. When the trains arrive at their **destination**s, the dabbas are given to the next team of dabbawalas. When the lunches are finished, dabbawalas will collect the empty dabbas and send them back through the same process. It is also much cheaper than eating out.

**Amazing! There is NO Technology in Dabbawalas system**

The delivery of dabbas, from beginning to end, is done without the help of the **technology**. Since most dabbawalas cannot read, they depend on a coding system using colors and patterns, which tell them which train to take or which office building to go to. The delivery system has an accuracy rate of 99.99 percent; that means there are only less than 4 **error**s in 1 million deliveries.

This system is so efficient that even Prince Charles, Richard Branson ,and employees from FedEx have visited dabbawalas and tried to learn how the system works the way it does. There are estimated to be around 5,000 dabbawalas in India. The numbers are still growing. What dabbawalas carry are more than just lunches. They carry the love and affection one family member has for another.

## Multiple Choices 小知識選選看

❶ According to the article, which of the following is not a reason why people use the dabbawala system?

(A) Having their lunches delivered costs less than going to a restaurant.

(B) People like having home-made food, and the food in a restaurant may not meet their needs.

(C) The government requires them to bring their own lunch to help protect the Earth.

❷ What does "dabbawala" most likely mean?

(A) A carrier of dabbas.

(B) A carrier of bicycles full of dabbas.

(C) Someone who eats from a dabba.

1 自然科學和科技

2 青少年生活

3 世界文化和歷史

4 現代發明

想像一下：在一條忙碌街道上，你看到一個戴白色帽子的男人在腳踏車上載著 30 個四層的午餐便當盒，他快速在交通中穿梭，來到火車站傳下便當盒。你看到的男人，是印度孟買最複雜且有效率的送餐系統裡重要的一環。

這個男人被稱為「達巴瓦拉」，因為他運送「達巴」，也就是在印度盛裝食物的容器，通常三到四層，由鋁製成。這些 達巴瓦拉 形成一個專門遞送午餐到辦公室或學校的神奇系統。過去在 1890 年代，孟買的餐廳很少，而在印度不同的族群與種姓階級各有自己的飲食需求，因為越來越多的白領上班族長途通勤上下班，回家吃比較想吃的家常菜是不可能的。因為想要吃太太煮的、熱騰騰的午餐，有個男人發想了這個遞送服務，這項服務後來演變成一個團體，在這個團體裡的 達巴瓦拉沒有老闆，並且他們會幫助彼此完成遞送任務。

**達巴餐盒在送達目的地前至少會經過三次轉運**

這套達巴瓦拉系統最神奇的地方是，一個達巴餐盒送達前至少會轉手三次。一大早，人們為自己心愛的人準備午餐，並把午餐放進餐盒。大約九點的時候，達巴瓦拉開始在自己負責的區域，一家一家收集午餐，他們跑上跑下，進入一棟又一棟的大樓。然後把全部的餐盒放上自己的腳踏車，這些腳特車是特製的，比一般腳踏車還重，因此有辦法承載很多餐盒，一位達巴瓦拉甚至可能載到 40 個餐盒。將近兩小時後，達巴瓦拉 便出發到最近的火車站，將餐盒交給下一組要去城市裡不同地方的達巴瓦拉，這組達巴瓦拉要在頭頂上的板條箱裝進多達 60 個餐盒，並設法找到對的火車。當火車到站的時候，餐盒又會被送到下一組達巴瓦拉的手上。最後，餐盒會在精準的時間送到對的人手上。等午餐用完後，達巴瓦拉還會將空的餐盒收回，經過同樣的程序，將它們送回家。這就是人們可以每天輕鬆拿到自家烹煮午餐的方法，這還比外食便宜許多。

**令人嘖嘖稱奇達巴瓦拉系統中沒有借助任何科學系統**

　　餐盒的遞送從頭到尾都沒有科技產品的幫忙，因為大部分的達巴瓦拉並不識字，他們使用顏色和符號做代碼系統，就可以看出要搭哪班火車或要去哪棟辦公大樓。這種運送系統的正確率高達百分之 99.99，這表示在一百萬次的遞送中，只會出現低於四次的錯誤。

　　這個系統如此有效率，連查爾斯王子、理查布蘭森以及聯邦快遞的員工都來拜訪達巴瓦拉，學習這個系統到底是如何運作的。在印度預估有大約 5,000 名達巴瓦拉，他們每天運送超過 200,000 個午餐盒，而數字還在不斷增加。這些達巴瓦拉運送的不只是午餐，他們運送的是一個家人對另一個家人的愛與關懷。

## ▶▶ 選擇題中譯

❶ 根據文章，以下哪個選項不是人們使用 dabbawala 系統的原因？

(A) 讓人遞送午餐比上餐廳吃飯更省錢。

(B) 人們喜歡家裡做的食物，而且餐廳的食物可能不符合他們的需求。

(C) 政府要求人們攜帶自己的午餐，以幫忙保護地球。

❷ 「Dabbawala」最可能是什麼意思？

(A) 運送 dabbas 的人

(B) 運送裝滿 dabbas 的腳踏車的人

(C) 用 dabba 吃東西的人

選擇題答案：1.C　2.A

1 自然科學和科技

2 青少年生活

3 世界文化和歷史

4 現代發明

# 3-9 Stereotypes and Discrimination
## 刻板印象和歧視

## Word Bank 刻板印象

| 字彙 | 音標 | 詞性 | 中譯 |
| --- | --- | --- | --- |
| generalize | `dʒɛnərəl͵aɪz | v. | 歸納 |
| train | tren | v. | 訓練 |
| avoid | ə`vɔɪd | v. | 避免 |
| experience | ɪk`spɪrɪəns | n. | 經驗 |
| positive | `pɑzətɪv | adj. | 正面的 |
| negative | `nɛgətɪv | adj. | 負面的 |
| prejudice | `prɛdʒədɪs | n. | 偏見 |
| common | `kɑmən | adj. | 常見的 |
| discrimination | dɪ͵skrɪmə`neʃən | n. | 歧視 |
| aware | ə`wɛr | adj. | 察覺的 |

**Word Bank**

# Reading—Stereotypes and Discrimination

 MP3 029

All Asian students are good at math. Women are terrible drivers. People in Egypt ride camels to school or work. These are some common stereotypes people have. A stereotype is an over-**generalize**d image of a group of people of the same race, nationality, age, gender, sexual orientation, etc. Our brains love stereotyping. However, certain characteristics one assigns to all people in a group are not always true and often are harmful. It is very important that we **train** ourselves to **avoid** relying on stereotypes.

**Why are stereotypes in the human brain?**

Every day, our brains are faced with millions of tasks to complete and decisions to make. It requires the brain to process things quickly. Therefore, our brains will form generalizations according to our **experience**s to help shorten the thinking process when facing similar situations. For instance, our brains will form stereotypes about bears so that we will run away when we see bears. The same thing happens in social interactions. We use stereotypes, some **positive** and some **negative**, as shortcuts that help our brains make decisions quickly when we are interacting with other people.

For example, when we need help to lift heavy objects, our brains will more likely tell us to look for a young man rather than an old lady because there is a higher chance that a young man can lift heavy objects. Such a mechanism saves our brains lots of time and energy.

## The bad effects of stereotypes in society

Even though stereotypes are natural to our brains, they may be wrong and can hurt people. When stereotypes are wrong, they become **prejudice**s and may cause hatred and damage. For example, a lot of people may think foreign workers are not well-educated or that they "steal" jobs from locals. These prejudices are not true at all. Prejudices like these are very **common** and, most of the time, are passed down from one generation to the next. If we act on the stereotypes and prejudices, **discrimination** occurs. When we treat foreign workers disrespectfully (不尊重地) because of the prejudices we have, we are discriminating against these people and treating them unfairly based solely (僅僅) on their nationality(國籍).

Discrimination can be seen on TV and in real life. People of color are often portrayed negatively in the media. Employers may deny women or older people's job applications and promotions. As mentioned, such discrimination stems from stereotypes and prejudices people have. To reduce prejudice and tackle discrimination, it is important for us to admit and be **aware** that we all have stereotypes. Remember, everyone is a different individual and it is very dangerous to judge people too quickly without really getting to know them.

## Multiple Choices 小知識選選看

_____ ❶ Which of the following is an example of stereotype?

(A) The owner of a store says he will not hire people who are homosexual.

(B) A taxi driver says he will not pick up some people because they are people of color.

(C) A teacher thinks that the boys in her class probably all like science.

_____ ❷ Why is stereotype necessary to our brains?

(A) Our brains dislike interacting with other people.

(B) Our brains need to shorten the thinking process to save time and energy.

(C) Our brains have to use up more time and energy.

_____ ❸ How can we avoid prejudice?

(A) We need to be aware of how we judge someone and spend more time to get to know the person.

(B) We need to blame ourselves when we find out that we have stereotypes about someone.

(C) We need to generalize more quickly when we are interacting with new people.

## ▶▶ 文章中譯

　　所有的亞洲學生數學都很好，女人車開得很爛，在埃及的人都騎駱駝去上學或上班。這些是其中幾個人們常有的刻板印象。刻板印象就是對一群有著相同種族、國籍、年紀、性別或性取向等的人過度概括的形象。我們的大腦非常喜歡建立刻板印象。但是，當一個人對一個族群裡的所有人套上某些特徵時，這些特徵並非正確，但通常很傷人。避免依賴刻板印象對我們是非常重要的。為何人腦存在刻板印象？

　　每天我們的大腦都要面對無數需要完成的任務、要做的決定。我們的大腦必須要快速地處理事情才有辦法面對這樣的情況，因此大腦必須根據過往經驗，做出歸納，以利往後面對類似的情況時，能縮短思考的過程，例如，我們的大腦會對熊形成刻板印象，我們看到熊的時候，才會知道要逃跑。同樣的狀況也會發生在社交互動上。正面或負面的刻板印象，在我們與人互動時，成為幫助大腦能快速做決定的捷徑。

　　例如，當我們需要找人幫忙搬重物時，大腦可能會叫我們找年輕男子，而不是年老的太太，因為年輕男子搬得動重物的機率比較高。這樣的機制可以省下大腦大量的時間和精力。

**刻板印象對社會帶來的負面影響**

　　雖然大腦自然會有刻板印象，刻板印象可能會是錯的，並會傷到其他人。當刻板印象是錯誤的時候，就形成偏見，引起仇恨或傷害。例如很多人可能以為外籍工作者沒有受過良好的教育，或是他們「偷」了本地人的工作，但這完全不是正確的。像這樣的偏見很常見，而且很多時候，會從上一代傳到下一代。如果我們將刻板印象與偏見實際表現出來，歧視就出現了，如果我們因為偏見而對外籍工作者不尊重，我們就是歧視他們，單純因為他們的國籍而不公平地對待他們。

　　歧視在電視上或實際生活上都有。有色人種在媒體上常被給予負面形象，雇主可能不把工作或升遷機會給予女性或年長的人。就像前面提到的，這樣的歧視就是來自人們有的刻板印象與偏見。要減少偏見與消除歧視，我們一定要承認並警覺我們有刻板印象。要記得，每個人都是不同的個體，在還沒認識一個人之前，就瞬間判定一個人是很危險的。

## ▶▶ 選擇題中譯

❶ 以下哪個選項是刻板印象的例子？
　(A) 一家商店的老闆說他不會雇用同性戀者。
　(B) 一位計程車司機說他不接送一些人，只因為他們是有色人種。
　(C) 一位老師覺得他班上全部的男生可能都喜歡科學。

❷ 為什麼刻板印象對我們的大腦來說是必要的？
　(A) 我們的大腦不喜歡與其他人互動。
　(B) 我們的大腦需要縮短思考的過程來節省時間和精力。
　(C) 我們的大腦必須用掉更多時間和精力。

❸ 我們如何避免偏見？
　(A) 對於我們如何評斷人們，我們需要更有自覺，並花更多時間了解一個人。
　(B) 當我們發現我們對一個人抱有刻板印象時，我們應該責怪自己。
　(C) 當我們和新的人互動時，要更快地概括歸納。

選擇題答案：1.C　2.B　3.A

# 3-10 The Mausoleum of Qin Shi Huang
## 秦始皇陵墓

 **Word Bank 秦始皇陵墓**

| 字彙 | 音標 | 詞性 | 中譯 |
| --- | --- | --- | --- |
| complex | ˋkɑmplɛks | n. | 建築群 |
| obsess | əbˋsɛs | v. | 迷住，使著迷；使煩擾 |
| vault | vɔlt | n. | 墓穴 |
| praise | prez | n. | 讚美 |
| dictator | ˋdɪkˌtetɚ | n. | 獨裁者 |
| tyrant | ˋtaɪrənt | n. | 暴君 |
| execution | ˌɛksɪˋkjuʃən | n. | 處死 |
| suppress | səˋprɛs | v. | 鎮壓 |
| immortality | ˌɪmɔrˋtælətɪ | n. | 永生 |
| unify | ˋjunəˌfaɪ | v. | 使成一體，統一 |

**Word Bank**

## Reading—The Mausoleum of Qin Shi Huang

MP3 030

When it comes to the most famous tomb **complex** in China, Mausoleum of Qin Shi Huang would be the very first idea come into our mind. It draws worldwide attention for two reasons. One is its complicated overall planning. The other is Qin Shi Huang's controversial role in Chinese history.

### Still Many Mysteries of the Mausoleum waiting to uncover

Until today, there are still mysteries of the Mausoleum of Qin Shi Huang waiting for archaeologists (考古學家) to uncover. This Mausoleum is a 76-meter-tall tomb complex located in Xi'an in northwest China's Shanxi Province. Since the accidental discovery in 1974, archaeologists have found about 7500 terracotta warrior and horses in the three tomb **vaults** they excavated. Amazingly, each of them had unique outlooks and the real size of a soldier is around 2 meters in height.

### The historical view of Qin Shi Huang

Historians judge Qin Shi Huang from many aspects. Being the first emperor of Qin Dynasty (221BC-207BC) and also of China, Qin Shi Huang deserves some **praise** for **unify**ing the warring China, the systems of laws and weights, and the Chinese written language. However, he is also as regarded a **dictator** or **tyrant** for the burning of the books

1 自然科學和科技

2 青少年生活

3 世界文化和歷史

4 現代發明

written by philosophers and the **execution** of the intellectual scholars to **suppress** opposition. Besides, he had hundreds of thousands of slave laborers construct the Great Wall. Believing in **immortality**, Qin Shi Huang was **obsessed** with finding an elixir of life to stay alive forever. That is why he forced 700,000 laborers to build the Mausoleum and buried 7,500 terracotta warriors there for guarding and protecting him in the afterlife.

## Multiple Choices 小知識選選看

❶ Until now, how many terracotta warriors have found in Mausoleum of Qin Shi Huang?

(A) 76

(B) 700,000

(C) 7500

❷ Why are Qin Shi Huang burning of the books written by philosophers and the execution of the intellectual scholars?

(A) To suppress opposition

(B) To find an elixir of life to stay alive forever

(C) To unify the systems of laws

❸ Which of the following is correct?

(A) All terracotta warrior have the same outlook.

(B) Qin Shi Huang is the second emperor in Chinese history.

(C) Qin Shi Huang forces hundreds of thousands of slave laborers construct the Great Wall.

1 自然科學和科技

2 青少年生活

3 世界文化和歷史

4 現代發明

## ▶▶ 文章中譯

　　一談到中國最有名的陵墓建築群，許多人腦中都會第一個浮現出秦始皇陵墓。秦始皇陵墓因為兩個原因而舉世矚目：一是本身複雜的整體規劃，二是秦始皇在中國歷史上實屬爭議人物。

### 秦始皇陵墓仍存在許多謎題尚待解答

　　時至今日，秦始皇陵墓中仍有許多謎團尚待考古學家解開其神秘面紗。此座 76 公尺高的陵墓建築位在中國西北方陝西省的西安。自 1974 年意外被發現後，考古學家至今已在挖掘出土的 3 個墓穴中發現約 7500 尊兵馬俑。令人驚訝的是，每一尊兵馬俑都具有獨一無二的外貌，高約 2 公尺。

### 秦始皇的歷史評價

　　史學家們從許多不同的面向來評價秦始皇。做為秦朝 (西元前 221 年~西元前 207 年) 與中國歷史上第一位皇帝，秦始皇統一戰亂的中國、法律、度量衡及中文書寫文字的貢獻值得讚揚；但由於他用焚燒哲學書籍與處死知識淵博的學者等方式來鎮壓異己，也有史學家視其為獨裁者或暴君。此外，他還下令數十萬奴工修築萬里長城。由於秦始皇相信永生，所以他十分著迷於尋找長生不老藥以獲得永生。這也是為什麼他強迫 70 萬勞工興建陵墓，並將 7500 尊兵馬俑埋於其中，以便在來生時守衛並保護他。

▶▶ **選擇題中譯**

❶ 時至今日，秦皇陵中共發現幾尊兵馬俑？

(A) 76

(B) 700000

(C) 7500

❷ 為何秦始皇要焚燒哲學書籍與處死知識淵博的學者？

(A) 為了鎮壓異己

(B) 為了找尋長生不老藥獲得永生

(C) 為了統一法律

❸ 以下何者正確？

(A) 所有兵馬俑外貌都相同

(B) 秦始皇是中國歷史上第二位皇帝

(C) 秦始皇強迫數十萬的奴工修築萬里長城。

選擇題答案：1.C　2.A　3.C

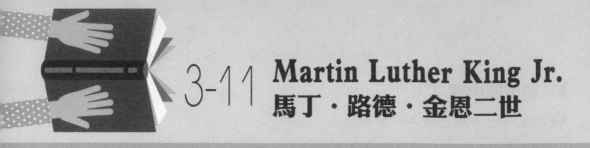

# 3-11 Martin Luther King Jr.
## 馬丁・路德・金恩二世

## Word Bank 單字

| 字彙 | 音標 | 詞性 | 中譯 |
|---|---|---|---|
| equality | ɪˋkwɑlətɪ | n. | 平等 |
| preach | pritʃ | v. | 鼓吹 |
| contribution | ˌkantrəˋbjuʃən | n. | 貢獻 |
| prejudice | ˋprɛdʒədɪs | n. | 歧視 |
| endeavor | ɪnˋdɛvɚ | n. | 努力 |
| prestigious | prɛsˋtɪdʒɪəs | adj. | 有名望的 |
| assassinate | əˋsæsɪnˌet | v. | 行刺、暗殺 |
| sentence | ˋsɛntəns | v. | 判刑 |
| innocence | ˋɪnəsns | n. | 無辜 |
| racist | ˋresɪst | n. | 種族主義者 |

Word Bank

# Reading–Martin Luther King Jr.

 MP3 031

When it comes to the important civil rights leaders who fight for the **equality** of African-Americans in American history, Martin Luther King Jr. is definitely the one who made the greatest contribution. Whether you know his story or not, he changed American society a lot in the 1950s.

Inspired by the doctrines of Christianity and Mahatma Gandhi, Martin Luther King Jr. **preached** non-violence in marches, strikes, and demonstrations against racial discrimination and segregation (隔離). In his famous soul-touching speech, "I Have a Dream," given in front of the Lincoln Memorial to huge crowds of whites and blacks, he told of a dream world where equality could be rooted in the American Dream and freed from racial **prejudice**. To this day, this talk is still regarded as one of the best speeches in American history. Owing to his sustained (持續不懈的) **endeavors**, he won worldwide recognition and was awarded the **prestigious** Nobel Peace Prize in 1964.

Ironically, on April 4, 1968, Martin Luther King Jr. was **assassinated** in Memphis, Tennessee by a **racist** and opponent of Dr. King's ideals named James Earl Ray. With sufficient and hard evidence, Ray was arrested and **sentenced** to 99 years in prison. However, until his death in prison on April 23, 1998, Ray had consistently maintained his **innocence**. Speculations had it that Ray could not have acted alone and was only part of a larger conspiracy (陰謀) by the government, either directly or indirectly. To honor Martin Luther King Jr's great **contribution** to civil rights, the US government set the third Monday of January each year as an American Federal holiday called Martin Luther King Jr.'s Day in 1986.

## Multiple Choices 小知識選選看

❶ Which way does Martin Luther King Jr. preach in marches, strikes, and demonstrations against racial discrimination and segregation?

(A) Violence

(B) Non-violence

(C) Not mentioned in the article

❷ What is the name of Martin Luther King Jr.'s most famous speech?

(A) I have a home

(B) I have a family

(C) I have a dream

❸ When did Martin Luther King Jr. win Nobel Peace Prize?

(A) 1964

(B) 1968

(C) 1998

1 自然科學和科技

2 青少年生活

3 世界文化和歷史

4 現代發明

## ▶▶ 文章中譯

　　談到美國歷史上替非裔美國人爭取公民平等權的重要領袖，馬丁•路德•金恩二世絕對是最具貢獻的那位。無論你是否聽過他的事蹟，他可是大大改變了 1950 年代的美國社會。

　　受到基督教教義以及聖雄甘地的啟發，馬丁•路德•金恩二世倡導以非暴力的遊行、罷工、和示威活動來對抗種族歧視和隔離政策。在林肯紀念堂前，他對著人山人海的白人和黑人群眾發表了著名且感人肺腑的演講：「我有一個夢想」，內容是闡述一個源於美國夢並且沒有種族歧視的平等美好世界。時至今日，這段演說仍被認為是美國歷史上最棒的演講之一。金恩堅持不懈的努力贏得全世界的肯定，他在 1964 年獲頒聲譽卓越的諾貝爾和平獎。

　　但諷刺的是，馬丁•路德•金恩二世在 1968 年 4 月 4 日於田納西州的曼菲斯遇刺身亡。兇手名為詹姆士•厄爾•雷，他是名種族主義者，同時也是金恩博士理念的反對者。由於罪證確鑿，雷馬上被逮捕，並被宣判 99 年徒刑。但到 1998 年 4 月 23 日雷在監獄內過世前，他都宣稱自己是清白的。人們猜測雷不可能獨自犯案，他應該只是政府直接或間接策劃的大型陰謀中的其中一員。為了紀念馬丁•路德•金恩二世對人權做出的重大貢獻，美國政府於 1986 年將 1 月的第三個星期一訂為名為馬丁路德•金恩紀念日的國定假日。

## ▶▶ 選擇題中譯

❶ 馬丁・路德・金恩二世倡導以何種方式進行遊行、罷工、和示威活動來對抗種族歧視和隔離政策?

(A) 暴力

(B) 非暴力

(C) 文章中未提及

❷ 馬丁・路德・金恩二世最著名的演講是?

(A) 我有一個家

(B) 我有一個家庭

(C) 我有一個夢想

❸ 馬丁路德金恩於何時獲頒諾貝爾和平獎?

(A) 1964

(B) 1968

(C) 1998

選擇題答案:1.B　2.C　3.A

1 自然科學和科技

2 青少年生活

3 世界文化和歷史

4 現代發明

# Part4 現代發明

　　「科技始終來自於人性，發明源自於人類需求。」我們身處一個便利又美好的世代，你是否曾經好奇身旁的「生活小物」的歷史呢？學校沒教，但其實很有趣的生活小知識，本篇共九篇，有可口可樂、花生醬、鉛筆到改變出版業的紙和印刷機，補充歷史課學不到，但其實大大影響人類生活的重要現代發明們，激發孩子們對生活的好奇心和發明魂。

# 4-1 Coke 可口可樂

 **Word Bank 可口可樂**

| 字彙 | 音標 | 詞性 | 中譯 |
|---|---|---|---|
| trademark | `tred‚mɑrk | *n.* | 商標 |
| formula | `fɔrmjələ | *n.* | 配方 |
| serving | `sɝˑvɪŋ | *n.* | (食物)一份 |
| pharmacist | `fɑrməsɪst | *n.* | 藥劑師 |
| solution | sə`luʃən | *n.* | 解決方法 |
| patent | `pætnt | *n.* | 專利 |
| popularity | ‚pɑpjə`lærətɪ | *n.* | 普及 |
| visibility | ‚vɪzə`bɪlətɪ | *n.* | 能見度 |
| lab | læb | *n.* | 實驗室 |
| painkiller | `pein‚kɪlə(r) | *n.* | 止痛藥 |

**Word Bank**

# Reading—Coke

 MP3 032

Though not all people like the marketing strategy of Coke, it is the best seller in the carbonated drink in the world for years. Coke is the **trademark** of Coca-Cola of Atlanta, Georgia. The name of Coke refers to the two main ingredients, kola nuts and coca leaves. These are the only 2 main ingredients that are published. The actual **formula** of Coke remains a secret. Some companies such as Pepsi try to recreate this drink, but none of them make it. Now, we can get a Coke in over 200 countries and people buy over 1.7 billion **servings** per day.

## The inventor of Coke – John Pemberton

John Pemberton, a **pharmacist**, chemist, and a businessman is the inventor of Coke. He established a drug business and owned several **labs** in 1955. The invention of Coke connects to his military days. In April 1865 in the Civil War, Pemberton served in the military and was badly wounded. To ease pain, he keeps using morphine like other injured soldiers. As a pharmacist himself, he knows it is not the **solution** and he started using his professional knowledge to work on **painkiller**s that would serve no opium. Then, Pemberton created the syrup and combined it with carbonated (碳酸的)water which was believed to be good for health back in

自然科學和科技

青少年生活

世界文化和歷史

現代發明

the 19th century and he believes this medicine would bring him to commercial success.

Pemberton claimed that Coke cured many diseases, including morphine addiction, neurasthenia, and headache. Later on, Frank Robinson registered the formula with the **patent** office. Pemberton even establishes his brand to sell his drug in Philadelphia, Pennsylvania. Unfortunately, Pemberton failed. Coke did not become popular until he passed away.

## The successful marketing strategy of Coke in 1891

The actual success of Coke came in 1891 after Asa Griggs Candler bought Pemberton's business. Candler decided to offer free drinks to people in order to raise the **popularity**. He also put the Coca-Cola logo on goods such as posters and calendars to increase the **visibility**. Because of his innovative marketing techniques, Coke became a famous brand and became a multibillion-dollar business. It is really hard to imagine that it was once sold for only 5 cents a glass.

## 👓 Multiple Choices 小知識選選看

❶ What is the main ingredients of Coke?

    (A) cacao nuts and cacao leaves

    (B) kola nuts and coca leaves

    (C) morphine and carbonated water

❷ What kinds of strategy that make Coke become successful suddenly?

    (A) free drink

    (B) put their logo on posters and calendars

    (C) all of the above

❸ Why did Pemberton make Coke in the first place?

    (A) to ease pain

    (B) to make money

    (C) to expand his business

**1** 自然科學和科技

**2** 青少年生活

**3** 世界文化和歷史

**4** 現代發明

儘管不是所有人都喜歡可口可樂的行銷策略，它可一直都是世界上賣的最好的碳酸飲料。可口可樂是位於喬治亞州亞特蘭大市的可口可樂公司的註冊商標。這個名稱來自於其中的兩個成分：可樂果和古柯葉，而這也是目前唯二公開的主要成分，確切的配方目前仍是個謎。許多公司如百事可樂都曾嘗試破解這個秘密配方，但無人成功。現在人們可以在全球兩百多個國家買到它，每一天的可口可樂銷售量更是超過了 1.7 億份。

### 可樂的發明者─約翰‧彭柏頓

可樂的發明人約翰•彭柏頓是名藥劑師，同時也是位化學家與商人。他於 1955 年創立了一個藥品企業，還擁有多間實驗室。可樂的發明跟他的軍旅生涯有關。在 1865 年 4 月的南北戰爭中，當時從軍的彭柏頓身受重傷。為了減輕疼痛，他跟其他受傷的士兵一樣，選擇不斷使用嗎啡。但身為一名藥劑師，彭柏頓知道這並非解決之道。因此，他開始運用所學嘗試研發不含嗎啡成分的止痛藥。19 世紀時碳酸水被視為是有益身體健康的，彭柏頓發明出一種藥水，並將這種藥水與與碳酸水混合，他相信這種藥可以為他帶來商業上的成功。

彭柏頓宣稱可樂可以治癒許多疾病，像是嗎啡癮、神經衰弱以及頭痛。後來法蘭克•羅賓遜替可樂的配方申請專利。彭柏頓甚至在賓夕法尼亞州的費城創立品牌銷售藥品。不幸的是他失敗了。可樂在彭柏頓有生之年並未流行起來。

### 1891 年可樂的成功行銷策略

1891 年阿薩•格里格斯•坎德勒收購彭柏頓的事業後，可樂才真的開始流行。坎德勒決定提供讓人們免費試飲的機會，使可樂更加普及，他更將可口可樂的標誌放在不同商品，例如海報與月曆上來增加品牌能見度。因為坎德勒創新的行銷技巧，可口可樂變得家喻戶曉，成為市值數十億美金的大企業，現在人們應該很難想像當初一杯可樂居然只要 5 美分。

## ▶▶ 選擇題中譯

❶ 可樂的最主要配方是？
   (A) 可可果和可可葉
   (B) 可樂果和古柯葉
   (C) 嗎啡和碳酸水

❷ 何種行銷策略使可樂突然大賣？
   (A) 免費試飲
   (B) 將商標置於海報和月曆上
   (C) 以上皆是

❸ 為何彭柏頓當初要發明可樂？
   (A) 為了止痛
   (B) 為了賺錢
   (C) 為了拓展事業

選擇題答案：1.B　2.C　3.A

1 自然科學和科技

2 青少年生活

3 世界文化和歷史

4 現代發明

# 4-2 LEGO
## 樂高

 **Word Bank** 樂高

| 字彙 | 音標 | 詞性 | 中譯 |
|------|------|------|------|
| **famous** | `feməs | *adj.* | 有名的 |
| **company** | `kʌmpənɪ | *n.* | 公司 |
| **carpenter** | `kɑrpəntɚ | *n.* | 木匠 |
| **founder** | `faʊndɚ | *n.* | 創立者 |
| **wooden** | `wʊdn | *adj.* | 木製的 |
| **produce** | prə`djus | *v.* | 生產 |
| **plastic** | `plæstɪk | *adj.* | 塑膠製的 |
| **design** | dɪ`zaɪn | *n.* | 設計 |
| **system** | `sɪstəm | *n.* | 系統 |
| **imagine** | ɪ`mædʒɪn | *v.* | 想像 |

**Word Bank**

**Reading—LEGO**

 MP3 033

A lot of people, young and old, enjoy playing with LEGO toys. The first LEGO brick was made over 50 years ago. Now the LEGO Company makes about 36 billion pieces of LEGO blocks every year. It is one of the most **famous** toy **companies** in the world. It all started from a **carpenter** from Denmark named Ole Kirk Christiansen. In 1932, the **founder** formed a company that made **wooden** toys. Later, he gave the company the name LEGO. The name came from the Danish phrase "leg godt," which means "play well." Ole's son, Godtfred, at the age of 12, helped his father with his business after school.

**The business history of LEGO**

The company grew bigger. Around 15 years later, LEGO bought a very expensive machine and started **produc**ing **plastic** toys, which included Automatic Binding Bricks, the earliest LEGO bricks. These bricks were only sold in Denmark and came in 5 colors. A few years later, the LEGO Group renamed the bricks and called them "LEGO bricks." The company kept making the bricks better and turned them into the LEGO toys we know today.

LEGO spent a lot of time to make sure that the material was right and the **design** was perfect. They changed the design of the blocks in 1958 and used a different material in 1964 so that the models people built could be stronger. The design of LEGO brick has remained unchanged since then, which means you can put together the bricks you buy now and the bricks you bought in 1958. Around the same time, Godtfred came up with the idea of putting the bricks into a **system**. With LEGO Systems, children could follow instructions and use the bricks to make airports, towns, or islands. Cars, airplanes, and figures were also included. Children could have fun and learn about these places at the same time.

Nowadays, whenever we hear the name LEGO, we think of the colorful building blocks that we can use to make anything that we can **imagine**. However, did you know that when the founder Ole started his company, he did not make any toys? At first, Ole sold wooden tools which people used at home. Sadly, times were hard and he had to let go of his workers. One day, he thought he could do something different and make toys that people and his own children could enjoy.

That was how he started LEGO. A fire and Ole's death did not stop the LEGO Group from making amazing toys that help make children and adults more creative. They are so popular that people from around the world use LEGO blocks to make short movies all the time. Today, we can even watch LEGO movies in theaters and play LEGO video games with our friends.

## Multiple Choices 小知識選選看

_____ ❶ Which of the following items was most likely sold in Ole's first shop?
(A) A wooden ladder
(B) A LEGO brick
(C) A plastic duck

_____ ❷ When did LEGO start making plastic toys?
(A) Before Ole had to send away his workers
(B) When people started making movies with LEGO toys
(C) After Ole bought an expensive machine

_____ ❸ According to the article, which of the following is NOT true?
(A) LEGO started as a company that made plastic toys.
(B) Children will not have problems putting together bricks they buy in different times.
(C) Thanks to Godtfred, children can play with LEGO toys and learn at the same time.

　　不論大人或小孩，很多人都喜歡玩樂高。第一塊樂高積木是在逾五十年前被製造出來的，現在樂高公司每年生產將近三百六十億塊樂高積木，是世界最有名的玩具公司之一。這一切都要從一位名叫奧萊・柯克・克里斯琴森的丹麥木匠說起。在 1932 年，這位創始者創立了一間製作木頭玩具的公司，後來，他將公司取名為「樂高」，這個名字是來自於丹麥語的「leg godt」，意思是「玩得好」。而奧萊的兒子古德佛德在十二歲的時候，便在下課時幫助父親的生意。

**樂高的商業歷史**

　　公司逐漸擴大，大約 15 年之後，樂高買了一台非常昂貴的機器，並開始製作塑膠玩具，其中包含了「自動組裝積木」，也是最早的樂高積木，這些積木當時只在丹麥當地販賣，而且只有五種顏色。幾年後，樂高集團幫積木改了名字，並叫它們「樂高積木」，樂高公司不斷改良他們的積木，成為我們今天所知的樂高玩具。

　　樂高花了很多時間來確定使用的材質是對的、設計是完美的，他們在 1958 年修改了積木的設計，並在 1960 年改變了積木的材質，人們用積木做出的模型才能更堅固，樂高積木的設計從這時候開始就沒變過，這表示你可以把現在買的積木和 1958 年買的積木拼在一起。差不多同一時期，古德佛德還想出了要把積木放在一起，形成一個系統，這表示孩子們可以依照說明，使用積木來建造機場、城鎮或是小島。車子、飛機和小人偶也包含在裡面。孩子可以一邊玩耍，一邊學習這些地方的相關事項。

　　現在我們只要聽到「樂高」這個名字，我們就會想到色彩繽紛的積木，我們可以用來建造任何我們可以想像到的東西。但是你知道嗎？創始者奧萊一開始創辦公司時，可沒賣任何玩具呢！一開始，奧萊賣人們在家會使用的木頭工具，很可惜的是，景氣不好，奧萊只好讓全部的員工離開。有一天，他覺得他可以做點不同的，並製作讓人們和自己的小孩可以享受的玩具。一場大火以及奧萊的死亡都沒有阻止樂高集團製作出美好的玩具，幫助小孩以及大人變得更有創意。樂高玩具受歡迎到世界各地的人們時常使用樂高積木來拍短片。今天，我們甚至可以到電影院去看樂高電影，也可以和朋友一起玩樂高電玩。

## ▶▶ 選擇題中譯

❶ 以下哪一個物品最有可能出現在歐爾的第一家店中？

(A) 木製的梯子

(B) 樂高磚塊

(C) 塑膠鴨子

❷ LEGO 何時開始製造塑膠玩具？

(A) 在 Ole 必須把他的工人送走之前

(B) 當人們開始拍攝樂高玩具的相關影片

(C) 在 Ole 買一座昂貴的機器後

❸ 根據文章，下列哪一個敘述不正確？

(A) LEGO 是一間以製造塑膠文具開始的公司

(B) 孩子們可以將他們不同時期買的玩具磚堆疊在一起

(C) 由於 Godtfred, 孩子們可以一邊玩樂高一邊從中學習

選擇題答案：1.A　2.C　3.A

# 4-3 Peanut Butter
## 花生醬

 **Word Bank 花生醬**

| 字彙 | 音標 | 詞性 | 中譯 |
|------|------|------|------|
| childhood | `tʃaɪld͵hʊd | *n.* | 童年時期 |
| dessert | dɪ`zɝt | *n.* | 甜點 |
| paste | pest | *n.* | 醬汁 |
| invent | ɪn`vɛnt | *v.* | 發明 |
| develop | dɪ`vɛləp | *v.* | 發展 |
| product | `prɑdəkt | *n.* | 產品 |
| well-known | `wɛl`non | *adj.* | 出名的 |
| spoil | spɔɪl | *v.* | 腐壞 |
| avoid | ə`vɔɪd | *v.* | 避免 |
| weight | wet | *n.* | 重量 |

**Word Bank**

# Reading–Peanut Butter

 MP3 034

Peanut butter can be said to be one of the most popular foods in the United States. Almost everyone has known and loved peanut butter since their **childhood**. According to the website Peanut Butter Lover, each American eats three pounds of peanut butter every year, which is enough to cover the floor of the Grand Canyon! People love peanut butter so much that they use it in different kinds of dishes. Not only do people use peanut butter to spread over bread, but they also dip celery sticks (芹菜棒) into peanut butter or make cookies and other **dessert**s with it.

### Where are the peanuts from?

It is possible that peanuts came from South America. Natives there first mashed roasted peanuts into a **paste** around 3,000 years ago. In the late 1800s, a few more people tried making peanut butter. A lot of people may think of an American inventor named George Washington Carver. However, he did not **invent** peanut butter, even though he did spend a lot of time looking for different uses for peanuts and **develop**ed **product**s from peanuts such as paints, soap, and glue.

The first person to claim ownership of peanut butter in 1884 was Canadian Marcellus Gilmore Edson, though he did not sell it as a product. As a pharmacist, he often saw people who had trouble chewing and swallowing food. He thought peanut paste could help these people get some delicious and healthy food. He also added sugar into the paste to make peanut candy. Afterwards more people got into the making of peanut butter and developed different kinds of peanut butter such as smooth, creamy, or crunchy peanut butter.

Different brands were also created, including one of the most **well-known** brands, Skippy, which was set up by Joseph Rosefield. He came up with a new process of making peanut butter that stopped it from **spoil**ing too quickly. This helped people get peanut butter more easily and thus peanut butter became even more popular.

You may think that peanut butter is just something you eat when you do not have time or when you feel like having something sweet. Moreover, after you eat peanut butter, you may not feel hungry for a longer time. Some people also use it to lose **weight**. Peanut butter is not only tasty but also healthy. Surprisingly, peanut butter is great for your health. It has a lot of nutrition and can help you **avoid** some diseases. You are less likely to have heart or memory problems if you eat the right amount of peanut butter every week. No wonder so many people love peanut butter and it is getting more fans every year.

## Multiple Choices 小知識選選看

_____ ❶ When did people have to be more careful when they wanted to say they invented peanut butter?

(A) 3000 years ago

(B) After 1884

(C) Before the 1800s'

_____ ❷ Why did pharmacist Marcellus Gilmore Edson come up with the idea of peanut paste?

(A) He thought it was the most delicious thing in the world.

(B) He wanted people who could not eat well to have some tasty and healthy food.

(C) He knew he could make a lot of money with it.

_____ ❸ According to the article, which of the following is NOT the benefit of peanut butter?

(A) Peanut butter can help you lose weight.

(B) You may have better eyesight.

(C) Having peanut butter can help you avoid memory problems.

## ▶▶ 文章中譯

花生醬可以說是美國最受歡迎的食物之一了，幾乎所有人從童年時期就知道並喜愛吃花生醬，根據網站「Peanut Butter Lover」，每個美國人平均一年就可以吃掉 3 磅的花生醬，這數量足以覆蓋整個科羅拉多大峽谷的表面！人們是如此熱愛花生醬，將花生醬用於各種料理中，他們不只用花生醬來塗麵包，更會將芹菜棒拿來沾花生醬或是用花生醬來做餅乾以及其他甜點。

**花生醬來自哪裡？**

花生可能是源自於南美洲，那裡的原住民在大約三千年前，最先將烤過的花生磨成醬。在 1800 年代後期，有更多人著手嘗試做花生醬，許多人可能會想到美國發明家喬治 華盛頓 卡爾弗。然而，他並不是發明花生醬的人，雖然他確實花了很多時間找出花生不同的用法，並從花生研發出不同產品，例如顏料、肥皂和膠水。

第一個在 1884 年申請花生醬專利的人是加拿大人馬塞勒斯·吉爾摩·艾德森 ，但他並未把花生醬當成產品銷售。身為一位藥劑師，他經常看到有嚼與吞嚥食物困難的人，他覺得花生醬可以幫助這些人嚐到一點好吃而且營養的食物。他還在花生醬裡加入糖，做成花生糖。

在這之後，更多人加入製作花生醬的行列並研發出不同種類的花生醬，例如滑順、綿密或顆粒風味的花生醬，不同品牌也創立了，包括最出名的品牌之一「吉比」，這是由喬瑟夫·羅斯菲爾德所創立的。他想出了一個製作花生醬的新方法，這種方法可以避免花生醬太快壞掉，這讓更多人能輕易地取得花生醬，而花生醬也變得更受歡迎。

你可能以為花生醬只是你沒時間或是想吃甜食的時候吃的食物。出乎意料之外的是，在你吃了花生醬之後，你可能會有較長的時間不感到饑餓，也有人會用花生醬減肥。花生醬不僅好吃，也對健康有益，花生醬其實對你的身體健康有許多幫助。花生醬富含豐富的營養，能讓你遠離一些疾病，每週吃花生醬的量若拿捏得恰到好處，可以降低你出現心臟或記憶力問題的機會。這大概是那麼多人熱愛花生醬，而它的愛好者也年年增加的原因吧！

## ▶ 選擇題中譯

❶ 人們在什麼時期要小心，不能隨便說是自己發明花生醬的？

(A) 3000 年前

(B) 1884 年之後

(C) 1800 年代以前

❷ 為什麼藥劑師馬塞勒斯・吉爾摩・艾德森會想要做花生醬？

(A) 他覺得這是世界上最好吃的食物。

(B) 他希望無法好好進食的人也能吃一些好吃又健康的食物。

(C) 他知道他可以藉此賺很多錢。

❸ 根據這篇文章，以下哪個選項不是花生醬的好處？

(A) 花生醬可以幫助你減肥。

(B) 你的視力會變得更好。

(C) 吃花生醬可以幫助你的記憶力問題。

選擇題答案：1.B　2.B　3.B

# 4-4 Ketchup
## 番茄醬

 **Word Bank 蕃茄醬**

| 字彙 | 音標 | 詞性 | 中譯 |
|---|---|---|---|
| brand | bræind | n. | 品牌 |
| sauce | sɔs | n. | 醬汁 |
| recipe | `rɛsəpɪ | n. | 食譜 |
| ingredient | ɪn`grɪdɪənt | n. | 食材 |
| harmful | `hɑrmfəl | adj. | 有害的 |
| customer | `kʌstəmə | n. | 顧客 |
| chemical | `kɛmɪk! | n. | 化學物質 |
| natural | `nætʃərəl | adj. | 天然的 |
| bottle | `bɑt! | n. | 瓶子 |
| quality | `kwɑlətɪ | n. | 品質 |

**Word Bank**

# Reading–Ketchup

 MP3 035

The most famous ketchup has to be the American **brand** Heinz tomato ketchup. Sometimes we dip our French fries in ketchup and sometimes you may add it to your hot dogs. However, ketchup's roots are anything but American. The name "ketchup" actually comes from a kind of Chinese fish **sauce**. The sauce made its way into other countries in Asia before it was brought to the west. During the journey, ketchup went through several changes. Surprisingly, tomatoes were not used at the time. Instead, people used fish, oysters, mushrooms or walnuts to make ketchup. The ketchup made earlier looked thin and dark. People would usually add it into soup, meat or fish.

## The problems of making ketchup

In around 1812, a scientist named James Mease showed people the first ketchup **recipe** that used tomatoes as the main **ingredient**. Tomato ketchup became popular. At first, people made ketchup at home or bought ketchup from farmers locally until bottled ketchup was sold commercially and nationally. Unfortunately, the tomato growing season was short and keeping ketchup from spoiling was not easy at all. Also, some producers handled ketchup poorly that the sauce often contained **harmful** things like bacteria or mold. To solve the problems, some producers used deadly preservatives, which were later banned.

## Henry J. Heinz becomes the name of ketchup.

Henry J. Heinz started making ketchup in 1876. Knowing that **customer**s would not want **chemical**s in their ketchup, he began producing chemical-free ketchup in 1906. Henry came up with a new recipe that used ripe, red tomatoes, which have a kind of **natural** preservative. He also increased the amount of vinegar used in the ketchup so as to lower the chance that the chemical-free ketchup would go bad. The Heinz brand dominated the ketchup market. In 1907, Heinz was producing around 13 million **bottle**s of ketchup every year and shipping a large quantity of ketchup to countries all over the world.

Henry J. Heinz did not start as a producer of ketchup. He started his business at a very young age packing and selling vegetables. His company failed at first, but he started another company in the following year. One of the company's first products was ketchup.

The product proved to be a success thanks to the fact that he insisted on using ingredients of the highest **quality** and came up with the brilliant idea of using clear glass bottles so that his customers can see the quality of his products. Today, Americans buy 10 billion ounces of ketchup every year.

When we use the word "ketchup" now, we mean a sauce that is made from tomatoes. We do not need to add the word "tomato" in front of it.

## Multiple Choices 小知識選選看

_____ ❶ Where does the name "ketchup" come from?

(A) It is similar to how the Chinese called a kind of fish sauce.

(B) It is similar to how the Chinese called fish.

(C) It is similar to how Americans called tomatoes.

_____ ❷ Why were harmful chemicals added in ketchup?

(A) The chemicals made ketchup more delicious.

(B) The chemicals made ketchup healthier.

(C) The chemicals kept ketchup from going bad quickly.

_____ ❸ According to the article, which of the following is NOT true?

(A) Ketchup comes from a kind of sauce made with fish.

(B) The American, Henry Heinz, was the first person to use tomatoes in ketchup.

(C) Nowadays, ketchup means a kind of sauce
that used tomatoes as the main ingredient.

## ▶▶ 文章中譯

　　最有名的番茄醬非美國品牌亨氏番茄醬莫屬，但是番茄醬的起源絕非來自美國。「Ketchup」這個名字其實來自一種中國的魚露，這種醬汁先被傳到亞洲其他國家，接著又被帶到西方。在途中，「ketchup」經歷了幾次變化；意料之外的是當時並沒有使用番茄，而是使用魚、生蠔、蘑菇或核桃來做「ketchup」。先前的「ketchup」看起來不濃稠，而且黑黑的，通常加在湯、肉或魚等料理中。

　　大約 1812 年，一位名叫詹姆斯・米斯的科學家向眾人發表了第一份使用番茄作主要原料的番茄醬食譜，番茄醬變得十分受歡迎。起先，人們會在家自製番茄醬或是向當地農夫購買，後來瓶裝番茄醬問世了，且在全國各地販售。很可惜的是，番茄生長期很短，而保存番茄醬讓它不腐壞並不容易。此外，有些製造商處理番茄醬不當，導致醬料內經常含有如細菌或黴菌等有害的物質。為了解決這些問題，有些製造商會加入有毒的防腐劑，而這些防腐劑之後也被禁用。

　　亨利・約翰・亨氏在 1876 年開始製作番茄醬。他知道顧客不會想要他們的番茄醬裡含有化學物質，所以在 1906 年他開始製造不含化學物質的番茄醬。他開發了一種新配方，使用成熟並含有一種天然防腐劑的紅番茄，他也大量增加番茄醬裡使用的醋，來減少不含化學物質的番茄醬腐敗變質的機會。亨氏這個品牌主導了番茄醬市場，在 1907 年，亨氏每年製造大約 1300 萬瓶的番茄醬，並輸出大量的番茄醬到世界各地。

　　亨利・約翰・亨氏一開始並不是製造番茄醬的，他年輕時以包裝與販售蔬菜起家，並在後來和朋友合夥，雖然公司在 1875 年失敗了，但是亨利・亨氏並沒有放棄，隔年他與家人共同創立了另一間公司。公司最先推出的產品之一便是番茄醬，這項產品很成功，全因亨利・亨氏堅持使用最高品質的食材，並想出一個聰明的點子，使用透明的玻璃瓶讓顧客可以看到自己產品的優良品質。現今美國人每年要買一百億盎司的番茄醬。現在當我們使用「ketchup」這個字的時候，我們指的就是使用番茄製作的醬料，不需要在前面特別加上番茄兩個字來表示。

▶▶ **選擇題中譯**

❶「Ketchup」這個名字是怎麼來的？
(A) 這個名字和中國人稱呼一種魚露的方式很類似。
(B) 這個名字和中國人稱呼魚的方式很類似。
(C) 這個名字和美國人稱呼番茄的方式很類似。

❷ 為什麼以前番茄醬裡面要加對人體有害的化學物質？
(A) 這些化學物質讓番茄醬更好吃。
(B) 這些化學物質讓番茄醬更健康。
(C) 這些化學物質讓番茄醬不會很快壞掉。

❸ 根據這篇文章，以下哪個選項不正確？
(A) 番茄醬來自一種用魚做成的醬。
(B) 美國人亨利・亨氏是第一個將番茄用在番茄醬裡的人。
(C) 現在番茄醬是指一種將番茄當作主要原料的醬料。

選擇題答案：1.A　2.C　3.A、B

# 4-5 **Pencil**
## 鉛筆

 **Word Bank** 鉛筆

| 字彙 | 音標 | 詞性 | 中譯 |
|---|---|---|---|
| lead | lɛd | *n.* | 鉛 |
| material | məˋtɪrɪəl | *n.* | 材料 |
| ancient | ˋeɪnʃənt | *adj.* | 古老的 |
| tool | tu:l | *n.* | 工具 |
| graphite | ˋɡræfaɪt | *n.* | 石墨 |
| method | ˋmɛθəd | *n.* | 方法 |
| require | rɪˋkwaɪr | *v.* | 需要 |
| allow | əˋlaʊ | *v.* | 允許 |
| take off | ˋtek͵ɔf | *ph.* | 起飛 |
| royal | ˋrɔɪəl | *adj.* | 皇室的 |

**Word Bank**

# Reading–Pencil

 MP3 036

Despite the advances in technology, a lot of us still use pencils almost every day. One of the most important parts of a pencil is the pencil core, which we also call "**lead**" in English. Did you know that even though we still call them "lead," pencil cores are no longer made of this **material**?

## The history of pencil making

The **ancient** Romans used a kind of **tool** to write and such a tool could only leave a very light mark, though not readable. The writing tool was usually made of lead, which was in fact toxic. In 1564, people discovered graphite in Cumbria, England and realized that **graphite** could actually make a better writing instrument. What people write with graphite was much clearer and, unlike lead, graphite is not toxic. Cumbria proved to be the only place that could provide a large amount of good quality graphite. The material was exported to many other countries.

One small problem was that graphite was very soft and would break easily. To solve this problem, people probably wrapped graphite with string or sheepskin at first. Later, wooden casings were used.

As England was the only place that had a large amount of

自然科學和科技

青少年生活

世界文化和歷史

現代發明

high-quality graphite, a lot of countries depended on the material from England or the pencils made in England. These countries tried hard to find the replacement so they do not have to rely on England. A lot of such attempts failed. Finally, due to a war between England and France, a French painter and army officer, Nicolas-Jacques Conte, was asked to come up with a new way to make pencil cores. Conte mixed graphite with clay and then baked the mix. His **method** not only **require**d much less graphite but also **allow**ed producers to adjust the degrees of hardness and darkness. Conte's creation became widespread in Europe and formed the basis of today's pencil making.

**Pencil was brought into the USA and became the world's best.**

European pencils were brought to America by settlers and continued to be imported until America started making its own pencils in around the 19th century. The American pencil industry **took off**. Because of their outstanding production abilities, American pencil companies started dominating the market and became the world's best.

Also, painting pencils yellow, which made pencils more special, possibly started with the American pencil companies. It is said that after England ran out of graphite, people found a place near China that could provide the best graphite. As in China, only the **royal** family was allowed to wear yellow, the companies painted the pencils yellow to give a feeling of royalty.

**People still love pencil.**

Perhaps you may think that no one uses pencils anymore. Instead, people use computers and cell phones to take notes or send messages. On the contrary, quite a lot of people miss the feeling of holding a pencil, even after they leave school. Some people love pencils so much that they open shops just to sell pencils. It looks like pencils will be in our lives for years to come.

 **Multiple Choices 小知識選選看**

_____ ❶ Why did some European countries try to find new ways to make pencils?

(A) They did not want to be controlled by England.

(B) The graphite found in England was toxic.

(C) They couldn't wrap string or sheepskin around the graphite they got in England.

_____ ❷ Who was more likely the first person to paint pencils yellow?

(A) Ancient Romans who needed to use writing tools.

(B) A French painter who wanted to make pencils differently.

自然科學和科技 **1**

青少年生活 **2**

世界文化和歷史 **3**

現代發明 **4**

(C) An American businessman who made pencils and sold them to the world.

## ▶▶ 文章中譯

即使科技發達，我們之中有許多人還是幾乎每天使用鉛筆。一支鉛筆最重要的部分之一便是筆芯，在英文中也用「鉛」這個字來代表筆芯，雖然我們用「鉛」來代表筆芯，筆芯卻不再是用鉛做成的。

### 鉛筆製作的歷史

古羅馬人使用一種工具來書寫，但這種工具只能留下很淺的標記，輕微的痕跡並不容易閱讀，這種書寫工具通常由鉛製成，而鉛其實有毒。在 1564 年，人們在英格蘭坎布里亞郡發現了石墨，並瞭解到其實石墨比鉛更適合做為書寫工具，用石磨書寫的筆跡清晰許多；而且和鉛不同的是，石墨是無毒的。由於坎布里亞郡是當時唯一蘊含大量高品質石墨的地方，因此這種材料便被出口至很多其他國家。但有個小問題，石墨非常柔軟、很容易破碎。為了解決這個問題，人們一開始可能使用繩子或是羊皮包覆石墨，後來人們則用木頭外殼取代。.

因為英格蘭在當時是唯一一個可以取得大量高品質石墨的地方，所以很多國家都依靠英格蘭提供材料或是在英格蘭製作的鉛筆。為了可以不再依賴英格蘭，這些國家想盡辦法尋找替代物，許多次的嘗試卻都以失敗收場。最終因為英國與法國間的戰爭，同時身為法國畫家與軍官的尼古拉斯・雅克・康特受託找出製作筆芯的新方法，康特將黏土混入石墨後進行烘烤，他的方法不僅大量減少了需要的石墨量，還讓製造者調整筆芯的硬度與顏色深淺。康特的發明在歐洲傳開，奠定今日鉛筆製作的基礎。

### 鉛筆被帶入美國市場，美國變成鉛筆製造業的領頭羊

歐洲的鉛筆由殖民者帶入美國，並持續輸入美國，一直到約 19 世

紀，美國開始製作自己的鉛筆。美國的製筆業開始起飛，美國的鉛筆公司因著出色的製造能力，開始主導市場並稱霸世界。此外，將鉛筆塗成黃色，讓鉛筆變得更特別，可能是起源於美國的鉛筆公司。據說在英格蘭的石墨開採盡了以後，大家找到一個靠近中國的地方，那裡蘊藏最好的石墨。因為在中國，只有皇室家族可以穿黃色，於是這些公司把鉛筆塗成黃色，希望能帶來一種王室尊貴的皇家氣息。

**人們還是喜愛鉛筆**

　　你可能會覺得現在已經沒人要用鉛筆了，人們都使用電腦和手機來記錄事情或傳訊息。相反的是，還是有不少人，就算離開學校之後，還是會想念手拿鉛筆的感覺，有些人十分酷熱鉛筆，還開了專門販賣鉛筆的商店，現在你甚至可以用鉛筆種出植物。這樣看來，鉛筆還會在生活中持續陪伴我們好幾年。

▶▶ **選擇題中譯**

❶ 為什麼當時有些歐洲國家試著要找到製作鉛筆的新方法？

　(A) 他們不想被英國控制。

　(B) 英國的石墨有毒。

　(C) 他們無法將英國的石墨用繩子或羊皮包覆起來。

❷ 誰最有可能是第一個將鉛筆塗成黃色的？

　(A) 需要使用書寫工具的古羅馬人。

　(B) 一位想要用不同方式製作鉛筆的法國畫家。

　(C) 一位製作鉛筆並將鉛筆賣到全世界的美國商人。

選擇題答案：1.A　2.C

# 4-6 Paper 紙

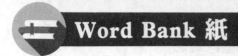

## Word Bank 紙

| 字彙 | 音標 | 詞性 | 中譯 |
|---|---|---|---|
| **deny** | dɪ`naɪ | v. | 否定 |
| **appearance** | ə`pɪrəns | n. | 出現 |
| **information** | ˌɪnfə`meʃən | n. | 資訊 |
| **bark** | bɑrk | n. | 樹皮 |
| **fiber** | `faɪbə | n. | 纖維 |
| **emperor** | `ɛmpərə | n. | 皇帝 |
| **important** | ɪm`pɔrtnt | adj. | 重要的 |
| **secret** | `sikrɪt | n. | 秘密 |
| **spread** | sprɛd | v. | 擴展 |
| **travel** | `træv! | v. | 旅行 |

Word Bank

##  Reading—Paper

 MP3 037

We may not be using as much paper as we used to be. More people are reading e-books rather than paper books. Credit cards and different e-payment methods are slowly replacing paper money. However, we cannot **deny** how our lives have changed with the **appearance** of paper.

Paper has come a long way since it was first invented. When paper history is mentioned, a lot of people would think of the papyrus used by ancient Egyptians. The use of papyrus dates back to as early as 4000 BC. Other writing materials, such as palm leaves, parchment, and vellum, were used in the same and other parts of the world to record **information**.

### Chinese paper inventor – Cai Lun

A lot of us have heard of Cai Lun being the inventor of paper. The paper as we know it today was first made in China by an official, Cai Lun, in 105 AD during the Eastern Han Dynasty. Though we do not know the exact materials Cai Lun used at the time, he most likely broke tree **bark** into **fiber**s and added them in water and possibly other materials. He reported his discovery to the **emperor** and was highly praised. However, you may be surprised to learn that recent discoveries suggest that Cai Lun may not be the inventor of paper. Paper made 100 to 200 years before Cai Lun has been found in China. Despite the discoveries, Cai Lun played an **important** role in the history of paper making. The paper made by Cai Lun had a better writing quality and could be produced at a lower cost because the materials were common in China then.

## How paper traveled around the world

Papermaking techniques remained only in China for quite a long time. China considered itself the center of the world and kept itself a closed country. Papermaking was finally brought to countries in Asia like Japan, Korea, or Vietnam. In 751 AD, some Chinese prisoners revealed the **secret** to the Arabs after losing the battle of Talas. This helped establish the papermaking industry in the Arab world. The Arabs kept papermaking techniques a secret from the Europeans. It was not until hundreds of years later that the technology was **spread** to Europe. The first European paper mill was built by the Arabs in Spain in 1150 AD. Finally, around 500 years later, North America had its first paper mill.

Something as thin as a sheet of paper has **travel**ed the world and made a great impact throughout history. Since its invention, paper has made recording and spreading knowledge easier and our lives more convenient with products like books, paper money, and toilet paper.

## Multiple Choices 小知識選選看

_____ ❶ Where was paper first invented?

(A) Egypt

(B) Europe

(C) China

_____ ❷ Why was the papermaking technique created by Cai Lun important?

(A) The paper made was more suitable for writing and cost less.

(B) The first writing material was created because of the technique.

(C) The technique created a large fortune for China.

_____ ❸ According to the article, which of the following is TRUE?

(A) The earliest writing material is papyrus, which is also the earliest paper.

(B) China shared the technique of making paper with the world right after the discovery.

(C) Chinese paper makers taught the Arabs how to make paper after they lost a battle.

我們現在不像以前用那麼多紙張了，越來越多人不閱讀紙本書，改看電子書，而信用卡與不同的電子支付方式也逐漸取代紙鈔。 雖然如此，我們還是無法否認紙張的出現，為我們的生活帶來多大的改變。

## 中國的紙的發明者—蔡倫

紙從發明到現在已經進展非常多。當談到紙的歷史時，很多人會想到古埃及人使用的紙莎草。紙莎草的使用最早可以追溯到西元前 4000 年，雖然英文字「paper」是來自紙莎草的英文「papyrus」這個字，但是紙莎草其實不是真正的紙，因為它的製成方式與紙張不同。在同樣的地區以及世界上其他地區，人們還會使用其他書寫材料來記錄資訊，像是棕櫚葉、羊皮紙和牛皮紙。

很多人都聽過蔡倫是紙張的發明者，現在我們所知道的紙張是在西元 105 年由中國東漢官員蔡倫所發明的。雖然我們不知道蔡倫當初確切使用的材料，但是他很有可能是把樹皮打碎成為纖維，再加進水中，可能還加入其他材料。他將他的發現報告給皇帝，並得到大力讚賞。

不過，下面這個觀點可能會令你感到很驚訝，近代的發現顯示蔡倫可能不是發明紙張的人。在中國已經發現一些紙張，是在蔡倫以前一百至兩百年間製成的。即使有這些新發現，蔡倫在造紙的歷史上仍然扮演了舉足輕重的角色，蔡倫製造的紙更適合書寫，也因為使用的材料在當時的中國更常見，因此製作的成本也較低。

## 紙如何環遊全世界

造紙技術有很長一段時間只在中國發展，當時中國認為自己是世界的中心，所以將國家封閉起來。後來，造紙術終於被傳到日本、韓國和越南等亞洲國家，西元 751 年，一些中國俘虜在輸掉怛羅斯戰役後，向阿拉伯人透露了造紙的秘密，這也使造紙業開始在阿拉伯世界生根。

阿拉伯人將造紙技術保密，不透露給歐洲人，直到幾百年後，造紙技術才得以傳入歐洲，第一間在歐洲的造紙廠是在西元 1150 年由阿拉伯人在西班牙建造的。又過了 500 年，北美洲終於有了第一間造紙廠。如此輕薄的紙張已經傳遍世界，並在歷史上帶來巨大的影響。自從紙張發明之後，記錄與傳播知識變得更容易了，而因著像書籍、紙鈔和衛生紙等產品的出現，我們的生活也變得比以往更加便利。

## ▶▶ 選擇題中譯

❶ 紙首先是在哪裡發明的？
(A) 埃及
(B) 歐洲
(C) 中國

❷ 為什麼蔡倫發明的造紙技術很重要？
(A) 這種技術做出來的紙更適合書寫，製作成本也較低。
(B) 這種技術做出了第一個書寫材料。
(C) 這種技術為中國帶來大量財富。

❸ 根據這篇文章，以下哪個選項是正確的？
(A) 最早的書寫材料是紙莎草，它也是最早的紙。
(C) 中國一發現造紙的方法，就立刻與全世界分享。
(C) 中國的造紙工人在輸掉一場戰爭之後教阿拉伯人如何造紙。

選擇題答案：1.C 2.A 3.C

# 4-7 **Photographic Film**
底片

 ## Word Bank 底片

| 字彙 | 音標 | 詞性 | 中譯 |
| --- | --- | --- | --- |
| film | fɪlm | n. | 底片 |
| camera | `kæmərə | n. | 照相機 |
| image | `ɪmɪdʒ | n. | 影像 |
| record | rɪ`kɔrd | v. | 記錄 |
| photo | `foto | v. | 相片 |
| equipment | ɪ`kwɪpmənt | n. | 設備 |
| chemical | `kɛmɪk! | n. | 化學物質 |
| develop | dɪ`vɛləp | v. | 沖洗（底片） |
| motion | `moʃən | n. | 動作 |
| capture | `kæptʃɚ | v. | 捕捉 |

**Word Bank**

# Reading–Photographic Film

 MP3 038

Most of the teenagers and kids nowadays have never seen or heard of this thing called "photographic **film**". Simply speaking, photographic film is a strip of special plastic that was put into a photographic **camera** to record still and moving **image**s. It was the main form of photography before digital photography started to replace it in the early 21st century. If a photographic film were not invented, we would not be able to see a lot of historic moments **record**ed and we probably would not have movies.

## The history of photographic film and its inventor George Eastman

To talk about the history of photographic film, we cannot leave out the inventor George Eastman. For the longest time, when people wanted to record the image, they had to rely on drawing or painting. Finally, photography was invented and improved. However, before George Eastman, taking **photo**s was for professional photographers. It required a lot of **equipment** and **chemical**s, and sometimes it took several minutes or even hours to take just one picture. Eastman decided to make photography easier. He devoted a lot of time to research even though he had never studied chemistry. After reading about the possible use of "dry plates," which would free people from bringing chemicals when taking photos outside, he decided to make his own. He succeeded and opened his own dry plate factory at the age of 26.

George Eastman did not stop there. He wanted to get rid of the heavy plates. In around 1885, he came up with the very first flexible paper film, which was light and allowed photographers to take many photos at a time. Furthermore, he thought he could make photography more available to everyone, people that were not professional photographers. He worked with a lot of people and made a much smaller camera for his roll film, the Kodak camera.

People could take up to 100 pictures with the camera. Once the film was used up, the whole camera was delivered back to Eastman's company and the pictures were **develop**ed. Now everyone could easily take photos themselves. Over the years, other companies and Eastman's company Kodak improved photographic film and developed several types of film, including roll film with paper backing, which could be handled in daylight.

In the 21st century, the photography market is greatly dominated by digital cameras. Not being able to transform itself early enough, Kodak was forced to file for bankruptcy around 80 years after its founder, George Eastman, passed away. Nevertheless, George Eastman and his company Kodak's inventions have forever changed the history of photography as well as that of **motion** pictures. The appearance of photographic film and the development in photography allow people to easily **capture** every precious moment they want to remember for a long time.

## Multiple Choices 小知識選選看

_____ ❶ How did people most likely take pictures in America before George Eastman's invention of dry plates?
(A) Children used a small camera to take pictures of their parents.
(B) A professional photographer used glass plates and chemicals to take pictures for his customer.
(C) A professional photographer took several pictures without changing plates.

_____ ❷ Why was the invention of roll film important to George Eastman?
(A) Using chemicals was too difficult.
(B) Dry plates were too heavy to carry.
(C) Developing photos was too challenging.

1 自然科學和科技

2 青少年生活

3 世界文化和歷史

4 現代發明

## ▶▶ 文章中譯

　　現在大部分的青少年與兒童可能從沒看過或聽過這個叫做「底片」的東西。簡單來說，底片是放在相機裡用來記錄靜態與動態影像的特殊塑膠長條片，這是在 21 世紀初期，數位攝影開始取代傳統攝影方式之前，主要的攝影方式。如果底片沒有被發明的話，我們可能沒辦法看到很多被記錄下來的歷史時刻，而電影可能也不會出現。

### 底片的歷史和它的發明者─喬治・伊士曼

　　如果要談底片的歷史，我們一定要談到發明它的喬治・伊士曼。長久以來，當人們想要記錄影像時，他們必須仰賴繪畫。終於，攝影被發明了，並被進一步地改良。然而，在伊士曼之前，照相是專業攝影師做的，需要很多設備與化學藥劑，而且拍一張照片可能需要花上好幾分鐘，甚至好幾個小時。伊士曼下定決心要讓攝影變得更簡單，雖然他從沒念過化學，他還是花了很多時間研究，伊士曼讀到可以使用「乾版拍攝」，而「乾版拍攝」可以讓人外出拍照時，不需要再攜帶化學藥劑，在這之後，他決定自己製作。他成功了，並在 26 歲的時候開設了自己的乾版工廠。

　　喬治・伊士曼並沒有因此而止步，他想要擺脫沈重的乾版。大約 1885 年時，他發明了第一個攜帶方便的卷式底片，非常輕便，也讓攝影師可以一次拍多張照片。此外，他還想到可以讓更多人可以接觸到攝影，也就是非身為專業攝影師的人。伊士曼曾和很多人合作，並為他的捲式底片做出一台更小的相機－柯達相機。

　　用這種相機，人們可以拍上一百張照片，等底片用光之後，再把整台相機寄回伊士曼的公司沖洗照片。現在所有人都可以輕鬆地自己拍照。數年間，其他公司以及伊士曼的公司柯達改良了底片，並發展出許多不同種類的底片，包含可以在日光下處理、帶有背紙的捲式底片。雖然在這之前就有彩色照片，柯達在 1935 年推出的柯達克羅姆底片可以拍出更美的彩色照片與電影。

　　在 21 世紀，攝影市場被數位相機給獨佔，沒能提早轉型。柯達在它的創辦人喬治・伊士曼過世後的 80 年後被迫宣告破產。雖然如此，喬治・伊士曼和柯達的發明還是徹底改變了照相和電影的歷史，而底片的出現和攝影的發展讓人們能夠輕易地捕捉每一個珍貴的片段，讓人可以將美好的回憶長存心中。

## ▶▶ 選擇題中譯

❶ 在喬治・伊士曼發明乾版之前，在美國的人們最可能是怎麼拍照？

(A) 小孩使用一台小小的照相機替父母拍照。

(B) 專業的攝影師使用玻璃版以及化學物質來替顧客拍照。

(C) 專業的攝影師不用換版，拍了好幾張照片。

❷ 為什麼發明捲式底片對喬治・伊士曼來說很重要？

(A) 使用化學物質太困難了。

(B) 乾版太重，攜帶困難。

(C) 沖洗照片太有挑戰性。

選擇題答案：1.B　2.B

# 4-8 Plastics
## 塑膠

 **Word Bank 塑膠**

| 字彙 | 音標 | 詞性 | 中譯 |
|---|---|---|---|
| pollution | pə`luʃən | *n.* | 污染 |
| way | we | *n.* | 方法 |
| occur | ə`kɝ | *v.* | 出現 |
| creation | krɪ`eʃən | *n.* | 創造 |
| succeed | sək`sid | *v.* | 成功 |
| explore | ɪk`splor | *v.* | 探索 |
| temperature | `tɛmprətʃɚ | *n.* | 溫度 |
| environment | ɪn`vaɪrənmənt | *n.* | 環境 |
| measure | `mɛʒɚ | *n.* | 手段、方法 |
| eco-friendly | `iko͵frɛndlɪ | *adj.* | 對生態友善的 |

**Word Bank**

## Reading—Plastics

 MP3 039

The Global plastic waste crisis is one of the most serious issues we face these days. We see piles of plastic bags at the dump or straws in sea turtles' noses. In fact, plastics materials are also used in products like clothes, erasers, and home insulation. Although plastic has caused different types of **pollution**s, it seems difficult to live without plastic because of its lower production costs and how widely it can be used.

### Why people started to use plastics?

It all started with a man named Charles Goodyear. At the time, natural rubber was used in many different kinds of products. However, people were troubled by how easily rubber would be melted in hot weather and become brittle (脆的) in cold weather. Goodyear had tried for a long time and finally accidentally discovered a **way** that would solve the problems. People started to use the material and the method in more products and the demand for natural rubber was overwhelming. Scientists had to look into new materials before rubber ran out.

The first man-made plastic was created by an Englishman named Alexander Parkes. Parkes's creation was very useful, but it still relied on naturally **occur**ring resources. A lot of efforts were put into making the **creation** better. Finally, in

1907, Leo Hendrik Baekeland **succeed**ed. He **explore**d different combinations of **temperature**, pressure and other factors and successfully invented Bakelite, the first fully synthetic plastic, meaning it was completely created by human beings and did not require natural resources. The material was later discovered to be able to take colors well, and its application became even more widespread.

The material could be found in buttons, furniture, telephones, and televisions. Bakelite officially led the world into the Age of Plastics. Since then, different types of new and better plastics have been developed.

**Plastics usage in the modern city and its problems**

Plastics are considered to be one of the most important inventions. We use plastics in so many things that it is impossible to imagine a life without them in the modern world. Sadly, the extensive use of plastics has become a serious threat to our **environment**. The plastics we throw away each year are enough to circle the world four times. Most of the plastics we throw away end up in the oceans and the problems are so serious that there are now new terms like "plastic soup" and "Great Pacific Garbage Patch".

People and governments around the world have realized how terrible the situation is and are taking **measure**s to solve the problems. The easiest things that people can do include avoiding single-use plastics, such as plastic bags and water bottles, and choosing plastic-free products whenever possible. Scientists are looking for more **eco-friendly** replacements for the plastics we use now and also ways to clean up plastic waste. Yet, it is time to use them responsibly.

## Multiple Choices 小知識選選看

❶ Which statement is the reason that plastics were invented?

(A) The materials used before plastics were causing environmental problems.

(B) Natural resources cannot keep up with the world's demand.

(C) A material that can take colors well was needed at the time.

❷ What does it mean when we say Bakelite is fully synthetic?

(A) It is completely made of plastics.

(B) It is made completely from natural resources.

(C) It is made completely without natural resources.

1 自然科學和科技

2 青少年生活

3 世界文化和歷史

4 現代發明

## ▶▶ 文章中譯

　　全球性的塑膠垃圾危機是當今人類所面對的危機中，最嚴重的危機之一，我們看到垃圾場一堆堆的塑膠袋或是海龜鼻子裡的塑膠吸管，你可能以為塑膠就是用來製作這些東西，但其實塑膠也用在如衣服、橡皮擦、居家隔熱等產品中。即使塑膠已經造成許多污染問題，但因塑膠生產成本較低廉，又能被廣泛應用，現在看來要擺脫塑膠似乎很困難。

### 為什麼人們開始使用塑膠？

　　一切都可以從查爾斯・固特異開始談起。當時很多產品都是使用天然橡膠製成的，但是有個問題讓人們十分困擾，橡膠非常容易在炎熱的天氣融化，也會因為寒冷的天氣而變得易碎。固特異嘗試了很久，最後終於意外發現了一個方法，可以讓橡膠不再有同樣的問題。人們開始將這個材料與方法用在更多產品中，對天然橡膠的需求變得十分驚人，科學家必須在橡膠用盡之前找出替代它的材質。

　　第一個人造塑料是由一位名叫亞歷山大・帕克斯的英國人所創造出來的，他的發明非常有用，但還是必須仰賴天然資源。很多人努力想讓這個發明變得更好，終於在 1907 年，利奧・貝克蘭成功了。他探索了溫度、壓力與其他因素的不同組合，並成功創造出酚醛樹脂，也就是第一個完全經由合成產生的塑膠，表示這完全是人造的，不需使用天然資源。在發現能幫這種材料順利上色之後，它的應用變得更加廣泛，在鈕扣、傢俱、電話和電視都能發現它的身影。酚醛樹脂正式帶領世界進入塑膠世代，自此之後，陸續發展出許多更新、品質更好的塑膠。

### 在現代社會中塑膠的應用和它的問題

　　塑膠被認為是最重要的發明之一。塑膠的應用廣泛到在現在的社會中，根本無法想像沒有塑膠的生活。可惜的是，如此氾濫的使用塑膠，已經對我們的環境造成嚴重的威脅。我們每年丟掉的塑膠足以環繞地球四圈，而這些被人類丟棄的塑膠大部分都會流入海洋中，問題已經嚴重到現在出現「塑膠濃湯」以及「太平洋垃圾帶」等新詞。世界各地的人與政府都開始意識到事情的嚴重性，並開始想方設法解決問題。我們最容易做的事包含避免使用一次性的塑膠製品，如塑膠袋或寶特瓶，並盡量選擇不含塑膠的製品。科學家也在尋找更環保的材質，來替代我們現在使用的塑膠，同時找尋清理塑膠垃圾的方法。但現在也是時候用更負責任的方式來使用它。

## ▶▶ 選擇題中譯

❶ 以下哪個敘述是塑膠被發明的原因？

　(A) 塑膠被發明之前所使用的材料會製造環境問題。

　(B) 天然資源無法跟上世界的需求量。

　(C) 當時需要適合上色的材料。

❷ 我們說酚醛樹脂是完全合成的，這是什麼意思？

　(A) 酚醛樹脂完全是用塑膠製成的。

　(B) 酚醛樹脂完全是天然資源製成的。

　(C) 酚醛樹脂完全沒有用到天然資源製成的。

選擇題答案：1.B　2.C

# 4-9 Printing Press
## 印刷機

## Word Bank 印刷機

| 字彙 | 音標 | 詞性 | 中譯 |
|---|---|---|---|
| carve | kɑrv | *v.* | 雕刻 |
| ink | ɪŋk | *n.* | 墨水 |
| mistake | mɪˋstek | *n.* | 錯誤 |
| character | ˋkærɪktɚ | *n.* | 字 |
| metal | ˋmɛt! | *n.* | 金屬 |
| wood | wʊd | *n.* | 木頭 |
| letter | ˋlɛtɚ | *n.* | 字母 |
| restrict | ɪˋstrɪkt | *v.* | 限制，限定 |
| rare | rɛr | *adj.* | 稀有的 |
| expensive | ɪkˋspɛnsɪv | *adj.* | 昂貴的 |

Word Bank

# Reading—Printing Press

 MP3 040

Can you imagine what it would be like if it took years to make textbooks for one class of 20 students? This was what life was like before the invention of printing. People had to copy every word by hand, and it might take months or years to finish one book. Nowadays, we can print a book in a few minutes and can easily print hundreds and thousands of books.

## The worldwide history of printing machine

You must have heard of Johannes Gutenberg as the one responsible for inventing the printing press. However, Gutenberg was not the first one to invent printing. China developed its printing process around 400 years earlier than Europe. At first, people, especially monks, **carve**d words on woodblocks and applied **ink** on the blocks to print a page of words or pictures on paper, like using one big stamp. This was the woodblock printing. Even though the technology became advanced and widely spread in Asia, it is very time-consuming and it is difficult to correct **mistake**s on a page.

Later in around 1040 AD (西元), movable type was invented by Bi Sheng of the Northern Song Dynasty. He carved **character**s on clay blocks and baked the blocks in the fire to harden them. Using this technology, people could choose the characters they needed and arranged them on a **metal** plate. These clay blocks with characters can be reused. Different materials, such as **wood** or metal, were used later. Nevertheless, this printing process was not widely used. Looking for the massive amount of Chinese characters is a very challenging job.

## Gutenberg's invention makes book-printing easily.

Woodblock printing (雕版印刷) was also used in Europe. Due to the establishment of the first university, books were needed. The existing printing process could not keep up with the demand. In 1439, German blacksmith, Johannes Gutenberg developed a more advanced moveable-type printing process (活字印刷). He invented the first mechanical printing press that used a special ink. Separate **letter**s were engraved on metal blocks, which were then arranged into words and sentences. He came up with a way to make letter blocks (字母塊) quickly. His inventions allowed books to be produced in a large number, around 3,600 pages a day and at a lower cost. The earliest newspaper was born thanks to the invention. In the 19th century, the rotary (旋轉式的) printing machine allowed 8,000 pages to be printed in an hour.

## Printing technology has never stopped progressing.

Before the printing press was available, books were very **rare** and **expensive**. With the invention of the printing press, along with the appearance of the cheaper writing material, paper, knowledge is no longer **restrict**ed to a very small group of people. Today, almost 2,000 years after woodblock printing was used, we have laser printing, which makes copying words and images more quickly and accurately, and even 3D printing, which prints chairs, food, organs, or anything you can think of.

## Multiple Choices 小知識選選看

❶ According to the article, which of the following does NOT describe movable-type printing?

(A) It was first developed by a Chinese man named Bi Sheng.

(B) It was extremely suitable for printing books that were written in Chinese.

(C) It made printing English books a lot easier.

❷ Which of the following is NOT true?

(A) Movable type was not very popular in China when it was invented.

(B) Gutenberg's printing press was a faster way to print books than the steam-powered rotary printing press.

(C) We can print a robot with 3D printing if we want.

## ▶▶ 文章中譯

　　你能想像如果幫一班 20 個學生製作教科書要花上好幾年，會是怎樣嗎？這就是在印刷術發明之前人們的生活，人們必須要手抄每一個字，完成一本書可能要好幾個月或好幾年。現在我們在幾分鐘內就可以印出一本書，也能輕鬆地印製大量的書籍。

**世界的印刷機歷史**

　　你一定有聽過約翰尼斯・古騰堡就是發明印刷機的人，但是其實古騰堡並不是第一個發明印刷術的人。中國大約比歐洲提早 400 年發展出自己的印刷技術。一開始，人們，主要是和尚在木板上刻字，塗上墨水之後，再像使用一個大印章一樣，將一整頁的字或圖印在紙上，這就是雕版印刷。雖然這個技術變得更進步，也廣泛傳到亞洲各地，此技術卻很耗費時間，頁面上有錯誤也不方便修改。

　　後來大約在西元 1040 年，北宋的畢昇發明了活字印刷。他將字刻在泥塊上，再放入火中烘烤，讓泥塊變得堅固。利用這項技術，人們可以選擇需要的字，將它們排列在鐵版上。這些刻有字的泥塊可以被重複使用，後來其他如木頭或金屬等的材料也被拿來使用。然而，這項印刷技術卻沒有被普遍使用，因為中文字的數量龐大，尋找字體成為一件非常有挑戰性的工作。

**古騰堡的發明讓書籍印製更容易。**

　　歐洲同樣也使用雕版印刷。在第一間大學被設立之後，對書本的需求增加，但當時有的印刷技術卻跟不上大量的需求。終於，有個男人想到了解決方法。在 1439 年，德國的鐵匠約翰尼斯・古騰堡，建立了更進步的活字印刷。他發明了第一台機械的印刷機，而這台印刷機使用的墨水是特殊的墨水。每個字母都單獨被刻在金屬版上，再排列成字和句子。他還發明了能快速製造這些字母版的方式。他的發明讓書籍可以被大量製造，一天約 3,600 頁，而且製造的成本較低，而最早的報紙也因此誕生。在 19 世紀時，平版印刷與蒸汽動力輪轉印刷機被發明了，輪轉印刷機一個小時可以印刷 8,000 頁。

### 印刷科技持續進步中

在印刷機發明之前，書籍十分稀有且昂貴。有了印刷機，加上較低廉的書寫材料，也就是紙張，知識不再侷限於一小群人。印刷科技未曾停止進步，在雕版印刷出現後，過了近 2,000 年的今天，我們可以看到雷射印刷，讓印製文字與圖片更加快速與精確，甚至還有 3D 列印，讓我們可以印刷椅子、食物、器官，或任何你能想到的東西。

### ▶ 選擇題中譯

❶ 根據文章，以下哪個選項不符合對活字印刷的描述？
(A) 活字印刷首先由中國人畢昇所發明。
(B) 活字印刷非常適合印刷以中文書寫的書籍。
(C) 活字印刷讓印刷英文書變得更加容易。

❷ 以下哪個選項不正確？
(A) 活版印刷在剛發明時，它在中國不是很受歡迎。
(B) 古騰堡發明的印刷機比起蒸汽動力輪轉印刷機更能更快的印製書籍。
(C) 如果我們想要的話，可以使用 3D 印刷印出一隻機器人。

選擇題答案：1. B　2. B

自然科學和科技　1

青少年生活　2

世界文化和歷史　3

現代發明　4

國家圖書館出版品預行編目(CIP)資料

我的第一本百科親子英語 / 郭玥慧著. - 初版
. -- 臺北市：倍斯特, 2019.01　面；
公分. --（文法生活英語系列；8）
ISBN 978-986-97075-2-7（平裝附光碟）
1.英語 2.學習方法 3.親子

805.1　　　　　　　　　　107017847

文法/生活英語　008

# 我的第一本百科親子英語(附MP3)

| | | |
|---|---|---|
| 初　　版 | 2019年1月 | |
| 定　　價 | 新台幣399元 | |

| | | |
|---|---|---|
| 作　　者 | 郭玥慧　邱佳翔 | |
| 出　　版 | 倍斯特出版事業有限公司 | |
| 發 行 人 | 周瑞德 | |
| 電　　話 | 886-2-2351-2007 | |
| 傳　　真 | 886-2-2351-0887 | |
| 地　　址 | 100 台北市中正區福州街1號10樓之2 | |
| E - m a i l | best.books.service@gmail.com | |
| 官　　網 | www.bestbookstw.com | |
| 執行總監 | 齊心瑀 | |
| 執行編輯 | 曾品綺 | |
| 封面構成 | 高鍾琪 | |
| 內頁構成 | 菩薩蠻數位文化有限公司 | |
| 印　　製 | 大亞彩色印刷製版股份有限公司 | |

| | | |
|---|---|---|
| 港澳地區總經銷 | 泛華發行代理有限公司 | |
| 地　　　　址 | 香港新界將軍澳工業邨駿昌街7號2樓 | |
| 電　　　　話 | 852-2798-2323 | |
| 傳　　　　真 | 852-3181-3973 | |